My First 7Days in Heaven
and more

My First 7Days in Heaven and more

ANDY SMITH

TKR Publishing
Nashville, TN

Book cover by Berta Martinez

Contents

Dedication

TO GOD

the only one I would
ever concede to creating a
better Heaven than I

I've watched Nova ya know.

Disclaimer

Please take note of the fact that I am not a theologian, I am not a Bible scholar, and quite frankly doing a bunch of research bores the hell out of me. If you are one of those religious people who feels the need to scour over this story to prove through exhaustive biblical references that my Heaven is unlikely to be anywhere near accurate, it will only prove that you are a bigger idiot than I.

I like my Heaven, and I do think that my Heaven makes sense. It takes the basic hopes that we all have when we think about Heaven – it is eternity, it gives you the opportunity to be with those you love doing the things you love to do with people still living on Earth, as well as those who have gone before you – and it does so without any consequences or negative outcomes.

As a religious man, I found myself going to church while I was writing this and smiling from ear to ear as I sat there contemplating my story. I realized that my Heaven is at it's very least a worse-case scenario. I am certain that God's Heaven is much better than what I have come up with. And that to me, is very exciting.

Introduction

I've said it before and I'm going to say it again.
For a creative writer, you only need two words
to get your adventures started... what if. Nothing
gets the creative juices flowing better than these
two simple words. My First Seven Days in
Heaven is a great example of the wonderful
world of what ifs. I had a dream. I don't put
a lot of stock in dreams. I've always felt that
dreams were just Gods way of entertaining us
while we're waiting to wake up. I never think
about my dreams. I never analyze my dreams.
I'm likely not to be able to tell you a thing about
my dreams after my first cup of coffee. But this
was just one of those dreams where you wake up
startled saying, "Wow ... that was weird."

I dreamed that I died and ended up in this
holding room where this guy was going over

everybody's name from a big book he was looking at. He passed out a sheet of paper with a bunch of lines on it and the words, 'Today, I'm going to___'. He explained that our Guardian Angel will explain the whole thing to us in the next room. And that's when I woke up.

After my first cup of coffee, my two favorite words began to do their magic. I started running the what ifs all over this dream and before my second cup of coffee, I was heading for my typewriter. I was having way too much fun with this idea to let it get away from me, so I started writing. I became obsessed with the whole idea and all the possibilities that came with every new adventure. I have no idea if anyone will appreciate this piece of work. I've written many stories and songs in my time, but this one is clearly the most fun I've had as a creative writer. With each day, I had to create new rules for Heaven that would make Heaven make sense. And once I got all those rules figured out, it simply became a fun adventure in living out my fantasies.

You may not get my first seven days in Heaven, but I'm hoping that you at least get the rules and start thinking what your first seven days in

Heaven might be. That's what makes 'what if' such a fun journey for us all.

Enjoy!

ASmith

1

The Arrival

I remember going into this room. There were a lot of people there. All different kinds of people. Different ethnic, styles and ages – though there obviously was no one under the age of thirty or so. Everyone seemed friendly, though a bit confused. I took a seat and there was a man standing in front of a platform with a big book lying open. He seamed to be reading the book and paid little attention to those of us coming in and finding our seats. It was a quiet, peaceful atmosphere. Everyone seamed to be as confused as I am, not knowing where we were or what was going to happen next. But as we all settled in, the man looked up and seeing that we were all ready, began to talk.

"Welcome. I am the keeper of the Book of Eternity. I will be brief in my comments as you will get a full explanation when you leave here of what to expect moving forward.

"First, you must understand that when you crossed over to this side, your soul, or heart if you will, went through what we call the wash. Everything that was negative in your life on Earth was washed away. You have no memory of pain, struggles or heartaches. You have no memory of people who treated you poorly or situations that happened which created a negative outcome. It's all been washed away. The only thing retained from the wash was love and the fruits of love. Every moment of your life where you felt love, comfort and happiness have been retained. All the people whom you loved have been retained. Every situation you had on Earth that brought a positive outcome has been retained. All these feelings, people and events will be very helpful to you on this side and serve as the foundation that you can build your eternity on.

"Second, please understand that I am the

keeper of the book. I am responsible for making sure everyone is here at their appointed time and that your name is permanently fixed into the Book of Eternity. Please do not ask me any questions. All your questions will be answered when you go into the next room. Keep in mind that when you crossed over to this side, time ceased to exist. There is no time on this side, so you have an endless opportunity to ask questions and pursue every possibility you can imagine. But you'll be doing that in the next room, not here, so please hold on to those questions and let me get through this process as quickly as possible so you can begin your hereafter.

"Now when I call your name, you will come up here and get this piece of paper (he holds up a piece of paper that seems to have few words and just a bunch of lines). You will take this paper and go through this door over here. (He points to a rather simple looking door to his side). When you go through this door, you will be greeted by your Guardian Angel. Your Guardian Angel has been assigned to you from the very point in your life when you began to formulate your own thoughts, desires and dreams – I think they call it puberty or something like that. Your Angel knows everything about you and will serve you in your eternity as a source and guide in developing your personal eternity. Your Angel will explain every detail of how this side works and the rules of how to develop your eternity. So as I call your name, please come up here quickly and get your piece of paper and leave through this door without asking any questions. Trust me, all the answers are on the other side of the door. I am merely here to make sure your name is secured in the Book of Eternity.

"Andrew Damien Smith"

I stand and go up front to pick up my piece of paper. The man smiles at me, checks my name off in his book and hands me the piece of paper. I look at it bewildered. There's broken lines at the top and about a third of the way down, it says, 'Today I'm going to__' and then the rest of the paper is full of lines. I look up at the man who smiles and motions me to move on so he can call the next name.

As I walk through the door, I am greeted by my Guardian Angel. Wearing a bright white robe, my Angel is smiling broadly and seems full of enthusiasm.

"Hi Andy. Welcome to the hereafter. My name

is Christopher, but you can call me Chris if you want."

"My Guardian Angel has a name?" I ask.

"Sure. Remember when you had your confirmation? You had to choose a confirmation name, right? Your confirmation day was the day I was assigned to you, so when you chose Andrew Damien Christopher Smith, I became Chris on this side. Good name, too."

"Does that mean that only Catholics have Guardian Angels with names?"

"Not at all. God gives all the Guardian Angels names, but since the Catholics choose a name at their confirmation, God thought it made sense to let that name stick with your Angel. Personally, God would be delighted if everyone else picked a name for their Angel as well and let Him go about other business, but it really doesn't make that much difference."

I am somewhat amused by this as I begin to look around. We are in what appears to be a huge library, which strikes me as odd, as Chris continues.

"This is the Resource Center. This is the base for your eternity. I have my office here and this will become a place for you to come visit often."

"It looks like a library to me." I say.

"It is. It has books on everything you can imagine. You can find the answer to any question here. And I know every page of every book. You can ask me any question and I'll be able to tell you exactly where to go find the answer. It's really cool and you'll see how great this place is as you learn more."

We get to another door and Chris opens it. It's a very simple room with a simple table and two large, very comfortable looking chairs on either side. Chris quickly moves to offer me a seat.

"Can I get you something to drink?" he asks.

"Gee, you can drink on this side, huh? Well, what do you have?"

"Anything you want, Andy. That's the nice part of being on this side. The first thing you need to learn is that there is no consequences over here. Remember, everything negative was swept away when you came through the wash. You can eat and drink whatever you like and you will never gain a pound, get heartburn or become drunk on alcohol. Everything on this side is created from the foundation of love in your heart. If you love cheeseburgers, you can eat them all you want and there will never be any consequences. There's no waste on this side. No restrooms, no diet menus, no hospitals, and no rehab facilities. You eat and drink whatever you want because it makes you feel good. No consequences over here," he explains.

Wow, I think, as I'm suddenly thinking this is going to be a very good place to be. Without asking a second time, Chris puts a drink in front of me that doesn't look very familiar. I take a sip and it is delicious. I'm surprised when Chris notices as he is sitting in his chair.

"You need to remember, Andy, that I have been with you since you were a teen. I know all your thoughts and have instant recall of your fantasies, desires and tastes. I am your personal library with instant access to every moment of your life. I don't really need to ask you if you want a drink or what you would like."

I'm a little uncomfortable that Chris knows everything about me, but again, Chris sees my concern.

"Also remember that all the bad stuff was washed away when you came over to this side. I still have access to the bad stuff, but only as a reference point to be used when and if needed. But let me explain how all this works and I'm sure you'll begin to understand as we go," he says.

"You get to create your own eternity. It will

come from the foundation of love that you brought with you from your life on Earth. It's pretty simple, really. Here's how it works.

"You will go through that door over there and find your room (he points to a simple door on the other side of the room). The room just has a bed and night stand because that's where you sleep. When you get up every morning, you take this sheet and decide what you want to do that day. At the top of the page, you list the people you want to see, and then you complete the sentence, Today, I'm going to__, and when you are done you simply go out your door and your day begins. There is no time here, so your day can be whatever you would like and last as long as you would like. When you have had enough, you simply come back to your room, go to sleep and when you wake up, the next day begins with you filling out your sheet again. Pretty cool, huh?"

Chris sees the hesitancy in my eyes and continues.

"Ok. Remember how you often fantasized about sitting on a cloud with Jesus and watching his whole life and asking him questions?"

Wow, he really does know my thoughts.

"That could be one day for you. Simply put

Jesus at the top, then complete the sentence; today, I'm going to sit on a cloud with Jesus where we can watch his life and I can ask him all those questions I've wanted to ask. When you open your door, you'll see Jesus sitting on a cloud ready to answer any questions you have. When you're done and have satisfied that fantasy, you simply go back to your room and go to bed. When you wake up, you can start a new day."

"Wow. Anything I want to do?" I ask.

"Sure. Remember, only love came through the wash. You can't hurt anybody and they can't hurt you. Each day can be whatever you feel like and last as long as you like. For instance, I know your girls were the most important part of your life on Earth. Over here, you can start every day off by going out to breakfast with your girls. Or you can spend a day with each one doing whatever you want. You could write down, today, I'm going to take my three girls to Disneyworld when they were 6, 8 and 10 years old. You can have their mother go with you if you want. Whatever. And you can set it up any way you want to."

"Wow. So can I go back to Earth and help my girls out through some rough spots?"

"No, you can't interfere with life on Earth. However, that reminds me of another part of the routine that you need to understand. Before you can start your day, you have to check your messages."

"Check my messages?"

"Yes. There will be a box by your piece of paper that has your messages every day. You must check the messages before you fill out your paper because the messages may dictate what you do for the day."

The look of confusion on my face brings a smile to his.

"You see, I know all the other Guardian Angels on this side. We keep in touch and pass along messages any time the situation warrants. Let's say one of your girls is going through a rough spot as you suggested. Her Guardian Angel would contact me and let me know. I would leave a message for you that your daughter is going through some tough times. You can't go back and solve her problems, of course, but you might choose to spend the day with her you know, and do whatever it was you and her enjoyed doing. You know how people sometimes will say, gee, I felt real close to my dad today? I felt as if my dad was with me. You know, stuff like that?"

I nod, " Yeah, I've heard people say stuff like that."

"Will there you go. That's what happens. You see, you may not be able to solve your daughter's problems, but by spending your day with her on this side, you'll serve as a comfort to her on Earth and she'll feel that closeness to you which may help to keep her strong in her tough time. That's why it's really important for you to check your messages every day before you complete your sheet."

"But how will I know if it helped her out?" I ask confused.

"You're always welcome to come here to the Resource Center. I'm always available. I can always get your daughter's Angel to sit with us and explain what's going on. We can see if maybe you need to spend the next day with her as well and come up with ideas of how to spend the day that would best benefit her situation. You always taught your daughters to listen to their hearts and that was excellent advice, my friend. The heart of love is always connected to the other side. As you spend the day with her, you'll know from her heart what her concerns are. And if she's listening to her heart, she'll feel the answers coming from your day with her.

That's why it's so important for people to trust their hearts. People who don't listen to their hearts miss out on many good messages coming from people who love them on this side. It's very frustrating as an Angel, I assure you."

I'm starting to understand how this can make a lot of sense to me. "Are there always messages?"

"Oh no, Andy. We always screen them and make sure you only get the messages that really need your attention. And it's not always bad stuff. You might get a message from your dad who is on this side asking you to be a part of his day. You can spend a day with anyone on this side by leaving them a message, or if you have a specific fantasy, you can just put it on your paper and go live it."

"Is there any difference?"

"A little. Say you want to meet your dad here at the Resource Center for a cup of coffee and plan out a day together in the future. If you just want to get together and plan a fantasy one on one, you would leave him a message and then you both are able to speak freely. Your sheet gives you the opportunity to fulfill specific fantasies that you have. The fantasies are driven by your heart, so it's your heart that decides what your dad says."

"Cool. So are there any rules to the fantasies you can fulfill?"

He smiles. "No sir, because we washed away all the things that would hurt or disappoint you. Besides, if you think about all the fantasies you had when you were on Earth, for the most part they were pretty positive, nobody got hurt and it was all very enjoyable. That's pretty much what you have here."

Wow. I hesitate as I'm a bit embarrassed to ask but dying to know. Chris smiles again as he knows.

"Yes, there is sex as well. It's a wonderful gift of intimacy that God has given you and over here, nobody ever gets hurt, no hearts are ever broken, and it's always very mutual and exciting."

"Wow. I know some guys who wouldn't have enough time even in eternity to satisfy all their fantasies."

"Well I'm sure there are a lot of men who come with a lot of sexual fantasies, Andy, but once you get into the many possibilities on this side, I think you'll see that sex really isn't that big of a deal here. Remember, you have an eternity. And there really is so much that you can do. Try a little of this and a little of that. It's kind of like an all-you-can-eat buffet. Take something and enjoy it. Have as much as you want. Then try something else. You keep bouncing around to all these wonderful flavors and textures and it's that wonderful variety and knowing that the food will never run out that makes it so satisfying. Sex can be a part of it, but I'm certain that you will come to realize that it's really not that important with all the other wonderful opportunities you have to create an exciting, fulfilling eternity."

Chris has really got me believing that I truly have gone to Heaven. But I'm not completely sure about all this.

"Does everyone come here?" I ask Chris.

"No. You have to have a certain level of love in your heart to come here. Obviously, after we wash away all the negative stuff, we need to be certain that there is enough good pure love in your heart to create a foundation that you can build your eternity on. Heck, if you wash away all the negative stuff in some people, there wouldn't be enough love in their heart to build an hour on, let alone an eternity of fulfilled fantasies. God has a place for those and all I can tell you is that God is very compassionate and even those people have opportunities to continue to grow and build the love in their hearts with hopes that they too, will someday be able to go through the wash and have enough love to build their own eternity."

"Cool. But what if you die young?"

"God makes provisions for those who die before they've had the opportunity to build enough love in their hearts. They are well provided for and God certainly takes care of them."

"That's cool." I hesitate in thought before I speak again.

"But what if I run out of things to do? What if I get bored with the whole thing? It is eternity, after all."

"Trust me Andy, you will never get bored here. That's what this Resource Center is for. Remember how you use to love to watch those science shows about the solar system and all the planets? Remember how many times you thought that when you died you hoped that you could go around to all the different planets and check them out?"

"Yeah. Hey, I could spend a long day doing that."

"Sure you can, but you can start here at the

Resource Center. There are more planets with activities going on than you can imagine. The scientists back on Earth have barely touched the surface of what is going on out in space. In here, we have every planet by name. You can read up on every one of them. You could build a day around each planet, exploring and observing everything about it. And that's just science. There are so many topics and stories in here. Trust me my friend, you will never run out of anything to do.

"And you might also remember that I have retained every minute of your life. You can always come to me for ideas. Remember how badly you wanted to be a baseball player? What if we took that day you threw your cleats in the trash because you didn't have enough confidence to compete. Why not go back there and try again – this time with all the confidence you need to win. You could build on that for a long time."

"Yeah, but if I made it in baseball, I might not have had my girls."

"Not so on this side, my friend. Remember, it's your fantasy. You create the story and you can make it anything you want it to be. The main thing to remember is that it all comes from your heart, and your heart is full of love and all the fruits of love. You will always have the capacity to create great and wonderful things to do.”

Chris has given me so much to think about. I almost don't know where to begin.

“Listen Andy, the best thing to do is just try it. Go lie down and think about it. When you wake up in the morning, pick something simple at first. Write it down on your paper, and go open your door. Maybe start with breakfast with your girls. Come back to your room and take a rest. Maybe next try a nice walk along the beach. As you try a few things, you'll be able to see how it all works and the more you get the hang of it, the more expanded your fantasies will become. And of course, you may wake up and decide to spend a day here in the Resource Center collecting ideas, or talking to me about your life on Earth. I'm always here and you can leave your fantasy at any time and come ask me questions. But if you trust and listen to your heart, I'm sure you'll work things out.”

“I suppose you're right. I could ask a million questions, but it might be better to just get out there and do it for a bit.”

“There you go. It's like baseball. You can talk strategy all you want, but it's better to just get out there and play the game and pick up the strategies from your experiences. Besides, remember – you can never get hurt. You can never fail. And I'm always here if you run into anything you don't quite understand."

With that, Chris leads me to the door that takes me to my room. It's a simple room, but comfortable and warm. I feel a very comforting peace as I walk in. I turn and see Chris smiling.

"Andy, there is so much to learn on this side. I'm certain that I have not told you everything yet. We'll let it evolve naturally. We'll learn as we go. It will all come together, you'll see. I know your heart. It's going to be a great eternity working with you. I'm here if you need anything."

He closes the door as I start my new life as a fantasy fulfiller.

2

My First Day

It took me a while to get to sleep – that's a lot of information to process after all. After sitting on my bed trying to process everything I have heard, I finally lay down to sleep thinking about all Chris had said. But I am surprised as I lay down how quickly I fade into a deep and peaceful sleep.

When I wake up the next morning, I decide that my first fantasy would be a simple one. I'm going to just have breakfast with my girls. After that, if everything goes well, I'm going to take a walk along the beach and think about other fantasies and maybe put them in order as I stroll along a beautiful beach.

I get up and take my sheet of paper. At the top, I write down, Tracy, Kelly and Rosemary. Then I write, 'Today, I'm Going To___' Have breakfast with my girls at a nice, relaxing restaurant.

I put my sheet down and hesitate as I make my way to the door. This is my first time, so I'm obviously a little nervous about how this is going to work. I put my hand on the knob, pause a few moments, then open the door, only to find myself standing in front of a brick wall!

Frustrated, I try to understand. I did what I'm suppose to do. It's a simple process, for crying out loud. My fantasy clearly was not to stand there looking at a brick wall!

I storm out the other door and into Chris' office, only to find him relaxed in his chair. He looks up and is smiling as if he knows exactly why I am there.

"My fantasy door is broken! I wanted breakfast with the girls and it gave me a brick wall!" I scream.

Chris stands up and he puts his arm around my shoulders.

"You didn't check your messages, did you Andy?"

The frustration drains out of me as I realize he is right.

"You can't leave the room until you check your messages. It's no big deal, just go back and check the messages."

"But this is my first day. How can there be any messages on the first day?"

Chris smiles at me, "Trust me Andy, it's a tradition. Go check your message and have a wonderful day. I'll be here if you need anything."

I'm a bit reluctant, but leave Chris and head back to my room. I go over to the box next to my paper and realize that it is blinking. It's probably some goofy greeting from all the Guardian Angels wishing me luck on my first day. I'm sure they just do that to make sure everyone understands that the messages have to be checked. I push the button that says, Check Messages.

'Andrew Damien, how's me boy doing? Welcome to the other side. Your Mom and I are outside waiting for you. I know you probably wanted to start in on your fantasies, but this is a tradition. Your first day is a family reunion. Your Mom and I will explain it to you when you come out, so just put 'Family Reunion' on the sheet and let's get this party started.'

I'm frozen. My Mom and Dad are right outside my door waiting for me. Now I'm really nervous. I write 'Family Reunion' on the sheet and head over to the door again, take a deep breath and slowly open the door.

As I peak around the door, I see Mom and Dad standing there arm and arm with big smiles on their faces. They look great and seem to be in a beautiful park of some sort. I quickly move out the door and into a big hug with my parents. I step back and look at them. They look so young – about forty or so. They look healthy and happy.

"We're so glad to see you, Andy. We've all been looking forward to this day. You're going to have a great time."

They take my hand and we start to walk towards a beautiful pavilion with a big, full tree hanging tall over it and it appears to be overlooking the ocean. There's a lot of people mingling about and I ask my Mom who they are.

"It's your family, Andy. Everyone who came here before you. Granny Dot and Panos, Grandpa and Mary Alice. Hermes, Ditty and Chuck, Carl and Mimi, Aunt Jean and Aunt Bobbie. Those relatives from your era are here, but after you've had time to visit with them, we are going to take you to another party with all the relatives from the past eras before your time."

I'm amazed as my Dad jumps in.

"This is how you start out on this side. You spend your first day with your family tree. You get to meet everybody and get to know them all. It's a great time. And it will certainly give you plenty of ideas for future fantasies. We've all had some great parties together. It's fun. We get together every now and then over a cup of coffee and decide what the next adventure will be. A bunch of us just got back from a week in Paris. It was the greatest."

I am totally excited as we close in on the party. Grills are smoking with the wonderful aroma of meat grilling, and there seems to be all kinds of food spread out. A bar in the corner with every imaginable beverage you could want. It's a beautiful setting. The perfect setting for reacquainting with those people I loved so much that left my life so many years ago on the other side.

"You all recognize my son, Andrew. This is his first day on this side, so let's celebrate and make him welcome," my Dad announces me.

I went to each one and got plenty of hugs. Dad brought me a drink, while Mom brought me a plate of food. I was so amazed at the love and the feeling of support for me. Everyone seemed anxious to visit with me. I noticed that everyone seemed to be young. My Dad told me at events like this the age doesn't really matter – you can pick the age you want to be. Everybody usually chooses to be in their prime, obviously. In fact, it seemed like Granny Dot and Panos were the youngest ones there. I brought that to Granny Dot's attention.

"Well I'm certain that your Grandfather – who is always 25- wouldn't want to hang around an 80 year old fuddy-duddy." She laughs as does Panos.

I am amazed at the love I see between the two. Panos died so early. My Mom explains that on this side, you can't choose to be older, just younger, so Panos and Granny Dot are pretty much staying in their mid-twenties. From what I see, my dear beloved Grandmother shows no signs of complaining.

Oddly, my Mom and Dad seem older than their parents, but there is little concern about this. Certainly on this side, age really doesn't matter. We are all just family. You don't get a sense that one is the mother of the other, or that one is the dad of the others. Everyone just seems to be good, close friends with no distinctive structure of family hierarchy.

It is a great feast. I have the opportunity to visit with everyone and there never seems to be any rush. Each relative explains how this side works from their advantage and everyone encourages me to include them in many of my future fantasies – a request I will have no problem obliging.

When I have visited with everyone, my Dad asks me if I'm ready to move on?

"Sure. Where are we going next?" I say with great enthusiasm.

Hermes points down the beach where in the distance I can see a huge gathering of people.

"That's the rest of your family. Here, you got to see those relatives that you actually knew during your life on Earth. But those are the family members that came long before your time. You'd be surprised who's in your family tree, Andy. Smiths, Panagiotopulos, Bainbridge, McDoughna, Lungren, Hicks, and so many more families. It's a great family tree and you're going to really get a kick out of meeting all these great people."

With that, we all head for the other party. There is great excitement as we go. Everybody seems to be telling me about the different people I'm about to meet. I can't keep up with all the information, of course, but I certainly get the picture. I'm getting ready for what I am certain will be a celebration of family like I have never imagined.

When we arrive, I look around at literally hundreds of people. You can clearly see the periods from where they came, but again, everyone is young looking and smiles are the norm.

I am introduced by Dad and am quickly handed another drink.

For the next eternity, I am greeted one by one by so many great people. Some of the names I had heard of before and was excited to put a real face to. Others I had never heard of but quickly became close to as they told me their place in my family tree.

I also noticed something that truly excited me. On the other side, I would have been very nervous in this setting, thinking that there was no way I could ever remember all these names and stories being thrown at me. But on this side, everything sticks. Instead of feeling overwhelmed, I am totally enthralled with all the people I am meeting and stories I am hearing. I have this great sense that everything I'm hearing is being retained. This is so exciting because I am quickly realizing that it's a good thing time doesn't matter on this side, as I am coming up with so many ideas for fantasies I want to explore after meeting all these wonderful people. I have so many family members that come from time periods that I always wanted to explore. On this side, not only can I do so, but now I can do so with members of my very own family tree. How exciting is that!

Well this day has totally blown me away. After meeting everyone and hearing all these wonderful stories, I am ready to go back to my room for a rest. It seems like everyone has made me promises to keep in touch and I have promised to include them in some of my future fantasies to be sure.

Wow. I'm exhausted, yet so excited I don't know if I'll ever be able to sleep. When I get to my room, instead of lying down, I head right out the other door to go talk to Chris and share with him all the wonderful stories this day has brought me.

I fly through his door and give him no opportunity to even say hello.

"Unbelievable! You would not believe the day

I just had. It was so incredible! I got to visit with my parents, grandparents, aunts, uncles. Wow! And then they took me to another party where I met members of my family I didn't even know existed! It was something Chris, and I'm thinking now that I might need an extension on this eternity stuff because I have so many new ideas to explore, eternity may not be enough time."

I stop to get my breath. Chris has the biggest smile.

"Well we find this is the best way to start. After you leave Earth, there are so many people thinking of you and feeling bad because you have left, we think it's good to send you on a family tree reunion until the emotions on Earth are settled down and we don't have so many messages to go through. Beside, you've got a great family tree Andy, and I can tell you won't be coming to me bored and looking for ideas any time soon."

I laugh, recalling how only yesterday I was asking him that question.

"Yeah. Man, I'm so excited, I think I'm going to have to grab one of these books out here to read before I go to sleep."

"Well you're welcome to grab a book any time,

but you also must understand that our pillows on this side are specially designed. As soon as your head hits the pillow, you have no problems going to sleep. But hey, that does remind me of something I need to show you."

Chris gets up and takes me out into the Resource Center and quickly guides me to a wall full of books. He looks at me and smiles. "You might want to start here."

I look closer at the books. Some of the titles are very familiar. As I gaze from row to row, the confusion on my face forces Chris to explain.

"These are all your stories, Andy. The books and plays you wrote as well as all the ones you never quite got to."

I look at Chris even more confused. "If I didn't get to them, how did they get done?"

"I wrote them for you. You had a pile of story ideas. You had notes for stories you wanted to develop. You had so many ideas that you could never even get them all written down as ideas. I took every idea and knowing you and how you write, I wrote the stories for you. It's your complete body of work, and I must say it's an impressive collection."

"Every story line I had is here and completed?" I'm dumbfounded.

"Yes sir. I know how you develop stories and I was able to complete everything. Go ahead and read one of them and tell me it isn't exactly how you would have written it."

I look back at the collection of books. Wow. So many titles I know instantly where the book titles came from. This is amazing.

"Too bad I couldn't have all this back on Earth."

"Earth isn't that important Andy. What is important is that it's all here for everyone to experience. The shelf life here is eternity. I think that beats anything back on Earth, don't you think?"

I select a book that I'm anxious to finally read. Chris sends me back to my room, assuring me that this was just the beginning of many wonderful experiences for me.

I am excited. It's been a great day. I have so much to think about. I am spent, and this is only day one of eternity. I lay back on my bed and flip open the book with great anticipation to see how my story line and this book are connected. It's then that I realize that Chris wasn't kidding. These pillows are special. The book will have to wait. I'm fading fast and ready to sleep, knowing that if my first day is any indication of what

Heaven is going to be, I'm certainly one lucky person.

God sure knows how to make a Heaven, that's for sure.

3

My Second Day

When I wake up the next day, I sit up in my bed and reflect on the family reunion. I'm thinking I'm going to go back to my first plan and simply have breakfast with my girls. I'm so inspired from yesterday, that I just can't wait to see them.

I go over to the stand and check my messages. Nothing there. Good. I grab my pencil and paper and write at the top, Tracy, Kelly and Rosemary. Then I complete the sentence. 'Today, I'm going to have breakfast with my daughters at a nice restaurant.' I go to the door – I'm not nearly as hesitant as yesterday – and open it. There they are – the most beautiful site ever created. They are busy talking as sisters do when they are young adults.

I walk in and am greeted with hugs and kisses as I settle into the booth with them. The muscles in my face are sore from my smile being so large and constant. I'm thinking eternity is going to be great.

As I start on my first cup of coffee, the girls ask me how I'm doing? I start telling them everything about the family reunion yesterday. I'm not missing a detail as my words are flying out faster than I can think them. As I move to the second party that has all the past relatives that I never met, I notice something that brings me to a curious halt. All three of my girls are just sitting there looking at me as if I'm the biggest idiot on Earth. I've seen that look from them before – mostly when they were teenagers. This is not what I was thinking of for this fantasy.

"Are you guys ok?" I ask.

Rosemary, never the shy one when it came to speaking her mind shoots right back. "Are you?"

I look all three of them in the eyes and realize that I have lost my girls. In a panic, I excuse myself and run right through my room to the door and into Chris' office. He is shaking his head.

"Hey! My girls think I've gone mad! That's not a fantasy!"

"Andy sit down. Maybe there are a few more points I need to give you before you really get the hang of this."

He pauses and offers me a drink – setting a cup of coffee in front of me because he's my Guardian Angel and thinks he doesn't have to really ask me.

"I don't want anything to drink, I want to know why my girls think I'm nuts!"

"Relax Andy, you're doing fine. We just need to go over a few details and you'll have the hang of it.

"First of all, you have to always remember that when you have a fantasy that involves people who are on the other side – still living on Earth – you have to have a fantasy that is within their frame of time. If you go out to breakfast with your girls, your fantasy has to stay within their world, not yours. You can create whatever fantasy you want, but it has to be on their side not ours. Any time you talk about this side, your words will be broken Latin and nobody will understand you – and your fantasy will default. It never happened. Is that clear?"

"Well it is now. Seems like that was some pretty good information I could have used beforehand. You're not very good at this are you?"

"We're fine, Andy. You'll get the hang of this in no time. Remember, there is no time on this side and only the positive love sticks on this side. It's all good."

I sit back and take a deep breath. Actually, what Chris says makes sense. I take a sip of my coffee and ask him if there is anything else I'm missing?

"Well Andy, let's just review the sheet once again to make sure. Remember now, when you write down the names of people who are still on the other side, you have to become part of the other side. Remember, it's a fantasy, so you can make it what you want, but it has to be within their laws of time. The trip to Disneyland when they were younger works. Telling them about the family tree reunion yesterday, doesn't work."

I nod now understanding from first hand experience.

"Next, keep in mind that if you write the names of people at the top who are on this side, they will be able to talk with you and participate in your fantasy as you wish them to. Your heart will guide their every word.

"Now, you could choose to just be an observer in your fantasy, and in that case you would not put any names at the top of your paper."

I look a bit confused as he continues.

"Let's say you want to go to the Yankee / Cubs game where Babe Ruth made the famous call for the home run."

I perk up. "Oh that would be cool."

"OK. If you simply want to see how it really happened, then you would not put any names at the top, you would just write, Today, I'm going to the Cubs / Yankees game to watch the Babe call his famous shot. You will open the door and be able to take a seat in Wrigley field and enjoy the game pitch by pitch. All the fans will be there but none of them will be able to talk to you or see you. You're just observing.

"Now say you want to go out after the game and have a drink with the Babe and talk baseball with him. Well then you would have to write down his name at the top of your paper. You can watch the game and then afterwards head down to the tunnel where the Babe comes walking out, recognizes you and the two of you can go wherever you want, sit and have a couple of beers and talk baseball all night long. Because the Babe is on this side, you can talk to him about baseball up to your day of passing. Everyone on this side understands everything up to the day of your passing. That actually would be a pretty good fantasy if you ask me.

"And finally, if you want to have a non-fantasy meeting with someone on this side you simply put the names of those you want to meet and then write, Today I'm going to meet with my Dad at an outdoor café in a non-fantasy setting so we can make plans for another fantasy. As you write, it automatically leaves a message for your Dad so he can speak freely because it's not a fantasy that you control. You'd be surprised how many times members of your family get together here at the Resource Center to plan trips. And they really put together a lot of great trips, too. They grab a bunch of books and go through them and wrestle with all the possibilities. Your family sure knows how to have fun."

I smile and nod. "There are no dull people in this family tree, that's for sure. So if I want to have a fantasy that involves people from the other side – still living on Earth – I need to keep the fantasy within their time limits and not cross over at any time to this side.”

“Right”

“If I want to simply observe something to see how it actually happened but don’t need to talk with anyone, I simply write the fantasy description and don’t put any names at the top.”

“Right again!”

“But if I want to talk with someone – who is over on this side – then I have to put their name at the top, and then complete the sentence and my heart controls what they say because it’s fulfilling a fantasy.”

“Correct again.”

“And if I just want to get together with someone and plan a future fantasy, I have to write that it is a non-fantasy setting and it will automatically leave a message for the other person on this side.”

“By George, I think he’s got it! And when it rains, where does it rain?”

I look at Chris unimpressed as he howls in laughter, relieved that I’m finally getting how this thing works. Reluctantly, I laugh too. But I’m anxious to go back and try breakfast again.

I excuse myself and head back to my room. I complete my paper again. Tracy, Kelly and

Rosemary. 'Today, I want to have breakfast with my daughters in a nice quiet restaurant.' I go over to the door and open it again to find my girls in the same setting. Once again I am greeted with hugs and kisses as I settle into the booth. I am more curious as I begin to make sure there is no sign of what happened earlier. They seem oblivious of my earlier ranting, so I'm thinking Chris got me straightened out ok.

It is a delightful breakfast. For the most part, I do what I always did before when I got together with my girls – I ate my food and pretty much sat back and watched them do all the talking. I always let them dictate the conversation, and given my earlier mishap, I was glad to let them do it now. They looked great and their spirits were so positive. It reminded me how much of Heaven I really had when I was back on the other side. I am so thankful that this side lets me experience this wonderful moment and am certain that I will enjoy this over and over again.

As we finish up, we go our separate ways. I of course go back to my room. Instead of resting, though, I want to go ahead and take a nice walk along the beach.

I check my messages – nothing there – and grab my pencil. 'Today, I'm going to take a nice walk along the sunny beach in the early morning hours.' I go and open the door and am stepping out on the beautiful beach.

I take a nice long walk, reflecting on so many things.

My family reunion and think about all the many possibilities I have to get together with them.

I go over the rules again and consider all the different scenarios of fantasies that I might want to explore.

But mostly, I just think about my girls. How great is Heaven when I can always find myself in the presence of those three girls.

I'm realizing that one of the hard parts about this side is controlling your excitement. I realize that it's important that we all have a room with a bed – and those special pillows to give us rest.

I head back to my room and lie down. I'm really enjoying this and am excited to see what tomorrow will bring.

As I thank God for my many blessings, I wonder if the girls are going to bed tonight feeling the same closeness to me that I feel for them.

I smile as I think that maybe Rosemary is

wondering where did Dad ever learn to speak
Latin?

I laugh myself to sleep.

4

My Third Day

I wake up and sit up in my bed. I reflect on what I have done so far and think about what I might want to do today. It's not a tough decision, as I already went through my wish list on my walk along the beach. Today, I want to go to my grandfather's office in New York City and see what it was like when he was a big time writer.

I get up and check my messages – nothing – Good. I grab the pencil and write at the top Paul Gerard Smith. I pause. Am I sure he's the only one I want to talk to back there? I shake off the thought. This is eternity after all. If I see anyone interesting, I can always hook up with them in a later fantasy. Today I just want to be with grandpa and see what his world was like when he was the great writer of Vaudeville times. I write, Today, I'm going to the W45th Street office of Paul Gerard Smith and spend the day talking to him about writing.'

I go to the door and open it. I walk into a nice lounge area with lots of chairs and couches scattered in no particular organization. It is clearly 1920 or so. Some of the furniture looks nice and expensive. Some looks like old stuff discarded by others and finding a new home.

As I walk in, I look to my right and see a large rehearsal hall with a piano, stage and big open wooden floor. There is a man playing the piano and a young lady singing next to him. They are working on new material. On the stage is a couple of young men that seem very focused on honing the timing of their routines. Off to the side is another man holding pieces of paper and discussing with another man what seems to be a change he is trying to make to the comic skit he is holding.

There are some people resting in the couches and chairs as I walk by, some talking and some sleeping. Ahead, I see a door wide open with a frosted window and the initials – PGS – stenciled on it. That must be grandpa's office. Typical that he would have his door wide open, as grandpa always welcomed a friend or family member to interrupt whatever he was doing.

I get to the door and peer in. Grandpa is busily typing away, smiling broadly as his fingers fly, throwing letter after letter at the blank piece of paper before him. He looks up and notices me and his fingers come to a screeching halt.

"Hey kid, come on in and make yourself comfortable. What brings you to my world? Can I get you a Dr. Pepper?"

He gets up and comes to me with a big hug. This strikes me as odd. Grandpa wasn't all that warm when I knew him back on Earth. I knew he truly loved his grandchildren, but I don't remember him be outwardly warm as he is now. I guess I didn't know him that well. I always just saw him as the old man. I never spent much time thinking that he might of had a life before he was the old man. But I guess that's the point of this fantasy.

"So this is where you work, huh?"

"This is it. The hub of Broadway. I have comics, singers and actors coming and going all day long looking for new material or trying to freshen up their old stuff. It's a lot of activity but I love it, kid. To spend your entire day with creative people bouncing ideas off the walls is one hell of a way to make a living. So what would you like to do today?"

"I just wanted to hang out here and see how the master creates his genius."

"Well kid, if a genius ever shows up here, I'll be sure to send you a message."

I laugh. Grandpa was always quick. Quick wit, quick at the typewriter and quick to throw out his opinions.

"Really gramps, I wanted to sit with you and talk to you about writing. I tried all my life to make it and didn't get very far. I know how hard it is to write really good stuff that nobody wants. I'd love to sit and talk to someone who actually made a living at it."

"Well don't sell yourself short, kid. I've read a lot of your stuff in the Resource Center and I'm telling you if you had been around during this era, you would have a big office like this as well. In this era all you needed was a good story and enough balls to never hear anyone say no to you. Except your grandmother – I always listened to every word Al said to me. I spent a lot of time talking to your buddy Chris and he told me all the stories of you trying to make it back on Earth. I'll tell you something, kid, you got the Smith gene for writing, but you got your mother's patience to be sure. I would have never been able to go as far as you did with all those silly rejections. You're a fine writer, Andy, and what happened back there only reflects the notion that the world has forgotten that the job of a writer is to simply tell a good story. Give 'em a good story and let them run with it and you create entertainment. The adventures Chris would tell me about you made me realize you never had a prayer. I guess good stories didn't hold much in your era."

He settles into his chair as I grab a chair and move it next to his.

"So when you write a story, gramps, what do you think is the most important ingredient?" I ask him, anxious to get into his writer's mind.

"People. It's all about people. You need to have a main character who is believable, and predictable. You want the audience to fall in love with him right away and know that they will love him throughout the show. Or you want them to hate him right away and know that they will hate him throughout the show. Then you surround him with other characters who create chaos, conflict and controversy. Of course, you need a story or your people just sit there laughing at you on your blank piece of paper with nowhere to go.

"Truth is, kid, the most important character in all my stories was your grandmother. Mary Alice was an angel and just thinking of her every day was enough for me. My stories always had to be great because Al deserved nothing but the best."

This is so exciting. Hearing my own grandfather talking about the craft I loved and tried so hard to master. And to hear him talk so lovingly about my grandmother I loved so much. This is a great treat for me.

We continue to talk writing for what seems like a flash and yet an eternity. We bounce ideas and stories off one another. I am totally blown away, taking every morsel of conversation and savoring every word my grandfather speaks. I truly am in Heaven and I could easily spend my whole eternity sitting here listening to this creative man tell his stories.

What strikes me as such a pleasant surprise is the mutual admiration we share for each other as writers. Grandpa is quick to ask me my ideas and listens intently to my every response. He laughs a lot. We both do. I would have thought that there would be a feeling of being way out of my league here. After all, my grandpa was a great writer during an era where writers ruled the entertainment business. Here I was with my writing resume that was admittedly not very impressive. I was Tiny Tim trying to fit in with the Mormon Tabernacle Choir. But instead of feeling inferior, we both were equal as we shared all our war stories, embracing our successes and laughing through our failures.

Every question created another. Every response created another story. I could see in his eyes that he was enjoying this as much as I was. I never looked at my grandfather like I did today. What a truly remarkable man. What a wonderfully creative mind. And what a truly loving and passionate man. This is the man I simply looked at as the old man for many years while we were on Earth. I see now how much I missed with that earthly vision, and I embrace this world of eternity where the opportunity comes to correct such shallow visions.

But we get to a point where we need to stop. I'm certain that he is anxious to get back to his loving wife and family. I am satisfied, knowing that on this side, there will always be opportunities to come back. Maybe new fantasies to explore with grandpa.

I thank grandpa for this incredible day and we promise each other that this was not the final visit. A warm hug from a man I have gained so much respect for... a man who has shown that he is so much more than an old man. He is a man that I am so grateful passed his wonderful genes my way.

As I enter my room, I am once again too wound up to think about sleeping. I don't have to think much, though. I know all too well what the best medicine for me is. I go to the desk and see that there are no messages and then I take the pencil to write. 'Today, I'm going to take a nice walk along the beach at the break of dawn.' I go to my door and step outside. This time a different beach, but still the great, wonderful tranquilizer my rushing soul needs after spending the day with grandpa.

It's a great walk. A calming walk that seems to help me sort everything out. The day with grandpa along with thoughts of what to do tomorrow.

As I head back to my room, I realize that a walk along the beach will likely become my personal bedtime story every night. I am refreshed and comforted. I am at peace with everything going on. I am ready to rest and excited in knowing that tomorrow starts another day. I thank God for letting me have this opportunity to see my grandfather in such a wonderful setting. I am spent. But I'm also completely satisfied as my heart is flowing in love and gratitude for the day given me.

I am thinking that my prayers on this side will consist of an enthusiastic redundancy of two words. Thank You. It's the only thing I can come up with when I start to pray. Thank you, thank you, thank you. If that's all you have to say when you pray to God, then you must be in Heaven.

5

My Fourth Day

When I wake up in the morning, I sit up thinking those pillows sure are great. It's hard to get use to the idea that time doesn't mean anything on this side, but I sure am beginning to understand that when I lay my head on those pillows, I am going to get a deep, peaceful sleep unlike any I ever had in my life on Earth. I feel great and refreshed.

I sit on the side on my bed thinking how I might want to start my day off. I know what I want to do today, but I'm also starting to get the hang of this place and feeling like I might want to try a few things out. Maybe I should start with a delightful breakfast down by the beach with the girls? Or maybe I could start the day with a nice baseball game Maybe I could give this sex thing a try? No, I'm not comfortable with that one. I know Chris is my Angel and is looking out for me, but sex with anyone I want? Sounds like a set up to me. You know, I think it would be great to have breakfast down by the beach with Jesus. Informal. I'd like to talk to him about some of the things in the bible and get his take on it. I'd love to see how things really happened back then. We could have a nice relaxing conversation, I would think. Yeah I'm thinking that would be cool.

I get up excited but also a little hesitant. After all, I'm going to ask for breakfast at the beach with the Savior of all mankind. Seems a little rude or imposing, I suppose, but I really would love to talk with him. It would be so fascinating to hear those bible stories directly from the man who lived it.

I go over to the desk and the message machine is blinking – I've got a message! Hey, maybe it's grandpa wanting me to hook up with him today? That would be cool. I push the Check Messages and it's Chris.

Hey Andy, your daughter Rosemary is going through a little rough spot right now . You might want to spend some time with her today.

I panic! Oh no, not my Rosemary! I fly through the door that leads to Chris' office and nearly dive into his lap.

"What's wrong with Rosemary? What's happened to her? What can I do to make things right for her?"

Chris looks like he just walked into a hurricane – and I suppose he did.

"Woe, woe, woe. Hold on there Andy. Let's sit down and relax, already."

"Relax?! You leave a message saying my girl is going through a rough time and you're telling me to RELAX!?!"

Chris is sitting back in his chair. He looks as if he has no intentions to respond to me. He's just smiling and staring at me!

"Well?! You know they may have washed away all the negative stuff when I came here, but don't test me on my girls 'cause I can gather up a whole lot of negative in a heartbeat!" My face is boiling red by now.

Chris shakes his head, smiling.

"Well Andy, your heart is certainly in the right place, I'll give you that. But I'm not going to respond to you until you are relaxed enough to listen to what I have to say, because you are not going to like what I have to say."

I blow up again. "What!?! Is she hurt bad? What happened? Whatever the bad news is I can handle it, but you simply can't tell me to sit down and 'R-E-L-A-X' when you tell me stuff like this."

"Andy PLEASE sit down. When I say you're not going to like what I have to say, I'm not talking about Rosemary, I'm talking about you."

"What do you mean you're talking about me? You leave me a message saying that I need to spend the day with Rosemary because she's going through a tough time and all I'm doing is asking you what the hell's going on so I can plan my day in a way that will help her out. Now what is so wrong about that?"

"Well there's nothing wrong with that really, but the problem is that I can't tell you what's going on with Rosemary until after you spend the day with her."

"Who came up with that rule? I mean what good will it do AFTER I spend the day with her?"

"It will be perfect because it will serve to validate the pure love in your heart for Rosemary and hers for you,." he says annoyingly calm.

I'm confused, but I have a feeling I better sit down and just shut up before I get myself in trouble, as Chris continues.

"Thank You. Remember when I talked to you about listening to your hearts? Remember how I complimented you on teaching your girls to listen to their hearts? Remember how I said that hearts of love are always connected? I want you to go back in your room and think about Rosemary. I want you to think of how you want to spend the day with Rosemary. I want you to be still and listen to your heart. Relax and trust your heart. Your heart will never lead you in the wrong direction. I promise you Andy, if you listen and follow your heart, you are going to be able to do so much more than if you come running in here screaming every time you're not sure about something."

He pauses as I take in what he has said. This is harder than I thought. He makes sense of course, but my concern for Rosemary without knowing what my concern is for is really tough. I get up reluctantly conceding and start for the door. Chris stops me.

"Andy, trust your heart. You have a great heart. That's how you got through the wash. Trust Rosemary's heart. You've raised her to be a wonderful woman with a strong and passionate heart. Let your hearts have this day. And PLEASE don't THINK. Don't get together with her and ask her a bunch of questions about what's going on. Remember, she doesn't understand Latin."

I smile sarcastically and shake my head.

"This isn't going to be easy you know. I mean can't you even give me an idea?"

"Andy, trust your hearts. In fact, I'm willing to bet that when you come back here after your day with Rosemary, you're going to be able to tell me what she's going through without me telling you. But only if you listen and trust your hearts."

I take a deep breath and start out the door, when Chris stops me again.

"Oh by the way Andy, the idea of having breakfast at the beach with Jesus is not rude or imposing at all. He'd be delighted."

I smile and am flushed with warmth as I turn and head for my room to consider what my next day will be.

I sit and start to think of Rosemary and as I do, I start to get excited. I get to spend an entire day with Rosemary. Wow! I could spend a whole day in the middle of a traffic jam with Rosemary and it would be a great day. But I have to think of Rosemary. What would she like to do? I remember the day I spent with her walking around Balboa Park when we all went back to San Diego. That was one of my favorite days ever. You know, Rosemary loves animals so much, I'm thinking maybe we should hook up at the San Diego Zoo and spend the day walking around there. She would certainly love that. But how do I know that's what she needs? Okay, I'm thinking too much again. I know she will love the day at the zoo and I just need to go with that.

I get up and go to write on my paper when I notice the message machine is blinking again. What's that all about? I reluctantly press Check Messages and it's Chris.

"Andy, the San Diego Zoo came from your heart. You're on track my friend. Have a great day and remember to let her start the conversations. I'll see you after your day.

I quickly write down Rosemary's name and then, 'Today, I'm going to spend the day walking around the San Diego Zoo with my favorite brunette, Rosemary!'

I move to the door and am anxious to open it and see Rosemary. I throw the door open and there she is, standing in front of a pond with a bunch of pink Flamingos walking about behind her. The smile on Rosemary's face melts me as

I quickly move to her and we embrace in a nice, long, warm hug.

We catch up for a bit – me desperately trying to avoid Latin and seeing that pained look on her face. Chris was right, though. By letting Rosemary start the conversations, I am better able to avoid any stupid mishaps like the first day we had breakfast. Rosemary is setting the pace and she sounds so excited. We get a map and plan out our entire day. And oh what a day it was.

Rosemary is my number three daughter. There were so few times I really got to be alone with her. This day really is a treat. I can tell it's a treat for her as well. We talk a lot. Actually, she talks a lot and I just respond to what she says. We stop and study every animal the zoo has and it is so clear to me that I definitely made the right choice today. We laugh a lot, tell stories and embrace every moment of the day. This is when I am so thankful that time has no impact on this side. I am in no hurry to see this day end, and I can sense that Rosemary is willing to test the rules of eternity as well.

But we finally end up at the pond with the Flamingos, having visited every animal and explored every corner of this wonderful zoo. It's time to say goodbye for now. We embrace each other in a long, warm hug that makes me almost feel as if we will squeeze each other into one being. I promise her many more days like this and I encourage her to keep following her heart. I thank her for being such a wonderful person and tell her how proud I am to be her dad.

We hug again and I turn to go back to my room. Of course, I bolt through my room and into Chris' office where he is waiting for me with his usual smile.

"Well how's Rosemary? Is she ok? Do I need to spend another day with her? What's going on?"

"Andy sit down! Relax. She's fine. Now remember, I said you could tell me after your day with her, so you tell me."

I stare at Chris in thought. Zoo. Animals. I got it!

"She got bit by a dog! Is she ok? Did she have to get shots? Tell me everything!"

Chris bursts out in laughter as I sit back a bit embarrassed and confused. I thought that was a pretty good guess but apparently not based on the laughter on the other side of the table.... Why, my Guardian Angel is practically in tears.

"No, no, no. Rosemary did not get bitten by a dog. She had to have a tooth pulled."

I sit back with pained confusion wrapped all over my face.

"WHAT!?!" I exclaim.

"Yeah, she had a tooth pulled and she was kinda worried about it."

We stare at each other desperately trying to sort this all out.

"So tell me this Chris, if she's in a wreck and is bleeding profusely from several parts of her body, what EXACTLY kind of day am I suppose to have then?!"

Chris shudders in horror. "Andy really, you shouldn't think like that on this side."

"Hey pal, I'm just asking. I mean Rosemary's a pretty tough cookie and I'm thinking her getting a tooth pulled would not exactly send her through a whirlwind of anxiety. It just seems like you're making a bit much out of one tooth. That's all I'm saying."

"Well that's true Andy, but you also have to remember that she is self employed. She works hard and is doing well trying to build a business and make ends meet. Now you know that Rosemary wasn't the best at handling financial struggles. She's not bad, but it's really not one of her strengths. It wasn't about the tooth, it was about her worrying about her struggling financially because she had to have this added expense."

I sit back and consider what Chris has told me.

"You know Andy, if you remember the conversations you had during your day at the zoo…"

I interrupt, "Hey you know, come to think of it, she did ask a lot of questions about the times when I struggled and how I handled it. Wow! It all makes sense now."

"Exactly! That's what I'm saying about listening to your hearts. You know, while you were walking around the zoo, she was under the gas at the dentists office and when she was, we were able to connect your day at the zoo with her heart and she was able to dream about it while you lived it in your fantasy."

"Really? How cool is that! The whole thing?"

"Yes sir. Next time you have a fantasy with her, it wouldn't surprise me if she tells you about the dream she had while she was getting her tooth pulled. Of course, it wouldn't surprise me either that you would jump right in and try to explain how the dream was all part of your fantasy in Heaven. And, well you know – the Latin thing."

"You're going to throw that at me every time aren't you?"

"Hey, this is eternity. I can ride that pony for a long time."

We both laugh. My laugh much less enthusiastic than his of course. But I am understanding more and it's making more sense to me with each day I have.

I'm ready to rest. But Chris isn't quite done with me.

"By the way, I see that you're thinking I'm just testing you about the issue of sex?"

Boy is he starting to scare me! He knows way too much.

"Well I don't know about all that. I mean it kind of makes sense I suppose, but really, it seems like a real selfish act for me. Having sex any time I want with any woman I want? It just seems to degrade what it's all about. I look at Mom and Dad. I watched Granny Dot and Panos. Grandpa and Mary Alice. I can see the love there and understand how sex would be a great part on this side. But randomly having sex with whomever I want doesn't seem right. I'm thinking it has to be special and that to be special, it has to be with that one true love of your life."

Chris smiles, "Your heart serves you well,

Andy. You know, that's one fantasy you've been avoiding."

I look at him, knowing exactly what he's saying, as I start to get up from my chair.

"Yeah well you're the one who said that the heartaches get washed away when you come to this side. I'm guessing that's a piece of Heaven I'll just have to do without," as I head out the door into my room.

"Remember Andy, this is Heaven. Listen to your heart and let your Heaven come to you."

I turn to Chris and smile. "Well you just let me know how Rosemary's tooth turned out, ok?"

Chris smiles and nods as I close the door and lay down on my bed.

It's been an incredible day. I've learned a lot and being with Rosemary today was absolute Heaven. I know that I will not wait for another message to spend the day with her. And certainly, Tracy and Kelly will also get their days. I think about that breakfast at the beach with Jesus and how Chris says Jesus would be 'delighted'. Tomorrow, I'm starting my day with that.

As I begin to fade, I think about what Chris said. That piece of Heaven that I'm avoiding. I'm wondering if my heart will ever be strong enough to approach that part of Heaven. I hope so, but I know that it will take a long time before I can trust that I can have that fantasy and only feel the love that I know is there. A love without any consequences. That would by my very best Heaven for sure.

6

My Fifth Day

When I get up, I know immediately how my day is going to start – given there are no messages, of course. I look and see that there are no messages – good – I write down Jesus, and then, 'Today, I'm going to have breakfast with Jesus Christ at a quiet beachfront resort.'

I go to the door and open it to find exactly what I was hoping for. A beautiful sunrise coming out of the ocean and there is Jesus sitting at a table taking it all in. I step out and move towards him and he smiles as he sees me coming. Suddenly I stop. It hits me that I am walking towards Jesus, the Savior of all mankind! The man who went through so much pain for me. The man who healed and made so many whole again in their hearts. I am suddenly overwhelmed and feeling that I have no right to be here with this great man.

Jesus understands and comes to me. I am certain that the expression on my face leaves no doubt about the fear and anxiety in my heart.

"Andy, I'm glad you came. I've been looking forward to this day for a long time."

I'm a bit uncertain. "You have?"

"Of course. Speaking to the multitudes never did much for me. I much prefer the one on ones."

I hesitate, but he guides me to my chair and we sit down to a wonderful table full of food and drink. I notice that Jesus likes his eggs sunny side up, which strikes me as oddly obvious. I still don't know where to begin or how to talk to Jesus, the Savior of all mankind. It's a bit awkward, to say the least. Jesus understands this and is quick to make me feel comfortable. He really knows how to help me relax and loosen up. I guess when you're the Savior of all mankind, figuring out stuff like this must be pretty easy.

By my second mimosa – Jesus does great wine drinks, that's for sure – I was beginning to be more comfortable and started asking Jesus those questions I had been hoping I could. I was amazed at how open and freely Jesus answered my questions. There was no sense of anything being off limits with him. Of course I was so moved by his passion and enthusiasm as he spoke. I thought there would be a lot of disappointment in how we humans have screwed so many things up back on Earth, but he was just the opposite. He spoke with a lot of encouragement and optimism.

I asked about times I've let him down or missed opportunities to do the right thing. Or all those times when my thoughts were less than pure.

He smiles, "Andy, those things don't come through the wash. You have to understand that the wash is the crucifixion. All the negative dies there. Only the positive comes to this side.

He picks up a rather thick book and hands it to me.

"Andy, this is your book of life that Chris and I went through before you came through the wash. Now I don't really need the book, but it might help you to understand the impact you had in your life that you may not realize. Your PIP number is really quite impressive."

I look at the book and then at Jesus, "My PIP number?"

"Yes, your PIP number is your Positive Impact on People number. In this book is all the people in your life that you had a positive impact on. The first section are all the people you said something nice to or made a nice gesture to, a simple act of kindness that made a very positive impression on them and made them feel good. There are a lot of people in this section.

Then in section two are the people that you had a significant part in turning their life in a positive direction. Maybe it was something you said, or something you wrote that really impressed them and with what others said or wrote, it was instrumental in turning a negative live in a positive, more productive direction. You have a very impressive number of people in this section.

I open the book and start to recognize names from my past life immediately before I look up at Jesus who is smiling at me.

"But the third section is the best. There are only forty-seven people in it, but these are the people you had a profound impact on. Your daughters are there, of course, but if you take the time to read them, there are some really good stories in this section." He pauses before he continues, "Remember that story you always told people about the girl you ran into at the strip club when you were delivering food?"

I raise my eyebrows in horror!

"You jokingly tell people how hard it was to keep your eyes at eye level when she was talking to you – she was a very attractive young lady to be sure – but what you don't realize is how hard it was for her to even approach you. She recognized you right away when you came in and immediately wanted to come say hello, but she was afraid that you would be so disappointed in her because she worked there. But you made such an impact on her when she was younger and you worked with her in the psych hospital, that she decided to take a chance. And YOU kept your eyes at eye level without judging her. YOU treated her like an old friend.

I have no response but am numb at what I am hearing.

"You know, Andy, that girl left work early that night, and after tucking her child in at bedtime, she sat in her bedroom and wept like she never has before. She prayed to me and said that if Andy believes in me without judging me, then I can believe and stop judging myself as well."

The tears are falling over the edge of my eyes as I had no idea I ever had such an impact.

"She quit being a stripper the next day, went back to school and do you know, Andy, that young lady is currently one of my best ambassadors of love that I have down there. A great mother, wife and one of the most positive people around." Jesus pauses to let it sink in. "Andy, she has done so well because you kept your eyes at eye level."

I sit back bewildered. This is way more than I even imagined. I look at Jesus who looks me straight in the eyes and smiles, "Thank You!"

"There are 47 stories like that in there Andy. If you ever question your being here, I want you to sit down and open this book to the third section. These wonderful stories are there because of you."

I am humbled. "I had no idea I had such an influence on anyone outside my daughters."

Jesus smiles, "Are you kidding? You had great impact on many people. You really should spend some time looking through this book that your life has created. It's very impressive."

I thumb through the book before asking Jesus what my PIP number is and how do they get it?

"Well you know how people down on earth

love their formulas and statistics. Of course, I don't need the formula as I know just by looking at your heart. But we start with your social number – it's the number between 1-10 that reflects the opportunities you had to have an influence on others. The Pope, Presidents and some movie stars have a social number of 1 or 2. People with a 10 social number had little or no opportunity to have an influence on anyone. You were a social number 7. You didn't have a lot of influence outside of your family and small circle of work and friends."

I hang my head a little, "Yea, I sure didn't make much of a name for myself did I?'

Jesus smiles, "Oh, that doesn't matter Andy. Your life was not about making a name for yourself. There are a lot of people who made names for themselves who may take several more lifetimes before they can get through the wash, believe me. You gave the writing a shot and it never took off. That doesn't mean much. I loved your writing."

I look up to Jesus who is smiling.

"So then we take a look at your book. The people in section 1 count as one point, the people in section 2 count as two and the people in your 3rd section count as 3. We add them up and multiply by your social number and that gives us your PIP number. Your PIP number was 152,992, which is a whole lot of positive impact in one's life if you ask me."

I look at Jesus unsure of what to make of the number.

"Numbers are not important, Andy. The important thing is to read these stories and understand the impact you had on people when you had the opportunity to do so. You really did a great job down there. We gave you one life and in return, you gave us forty seven wonderful, positive lives. No matter how you look at it, that's a pretty good return on your investment, wouldn't you say?"

"How's my number compared to others?"

Jesus laughs, "I don't compare, Andy. Your life was never in competition with anyone else's life. I really don't care about the numbers. That's just a formula that Chris and the other Angels like to use because they're into that sort of thing. Angels are a very competitive group, if you ask me. For me it's all about heart. And no matter how you look at your life, your heart served you well."

I take a sip of my mimosa as I consider all that Jesus has shared with me. I am certain that I am going to spend a lot of time looking through this book he gave me.

We talked about other topics too. Those questions I've always had in my life. We cover so many topics, and the more he talked the more questions I wanted to ask. It was an incredible morning. We covered so many topics and Jesus never seemed rushed or in any hurry to wrap this up. He even gave me some pointers on some of my future fantasy plans.

I get to a point where I feel the need to wrap this morning up. After all, he is Jesus, the Savior of all mankind and I really don't want to hog him all to myself for too long – even though he doesn't seem to mind. I don't know what to say to him except thank you. I thank him for everything and especially meeting me like this to talk to me. He is so warm and kind. He really makes me feel as if he would not have chosen any other way to start a day than this. He of course encourages me and tells me how well I'm adjusting to my new world.

He gives me a hug and I head back to my room. I sit on my bed. I am humbled at the experience but also completely satisfied. I'm not sure what else I should do today. I'm thinking it might be good to spend some time in the Resource Center and browse around. Jesus gave me some cool tips on some planets to look up that I might enjoy. That might be the best way to spend my day after a breakfast with the Savior of all mankind, after all.

It's then that I notice that my message light is blinking again. If Rosemary has to have another tooth pulled, I'm going to have to go against the rules and kill Chris.

Hey Andy, this is your Dad. Your Mom and I have a surprise for you. Just write down Today, I'm going to spend the day with Mom and Dad. Hurry up, we're waiting outside.

I do as I'm told and head for the door. I open it and there's Mom and Dad, dressed fancy and looking great! They are standing outside a large building – very artsy looking.

"Come on son, you're going to enjoy this one."

I head with them into the building and it appears to be a big concert hall. High ceilings, very eloquent and all the people seem very excited and anxious to go in and find their seats.

"Come on, we have our seats up in the balcony." my Dad seems so excited.

We climb the stairs and Dad opens the door leading into the concert hall. I am greeted by many familiar faces.

"We invited everyone in the family to join us and we filled up the entire balcony."

I make my way to my seat through many hugs, waves and greetings. So many of my family tree are here. This is great.

"So who are we going to see?" I ask Dad.

"Everybody who's anybody is performing tonight. Your Grandpa, Hermes and I put this show together and we thought you might enjoy it."

The lights go out and everyone settles into a quiet anticipation. Suddenly, the music crashes into a very familiar run. I know that crashing start by heart – I should because I wrote it! I look over at Dad who is smiling from ear to ear. I look back to the stage and the spot comes up on Billy Joel who starts singing I'll Keep The Coffee Warm Tonight exactly the way I heard it so many times in my head – if not better.

Dad leans over, "Your Grandpa, Hermes and I went over every one of your songs and matched each song with the perfect performer. Tonight, we're going to hear The songs of Andy Smith – done the way they were meant to be done."

I am speechless. I look around the balcony and see my family tree enjoying my songs. I look down on the floor of the hall and there are people everywhere, moving to the beats of my music.

What a surprise, indeed. One by one, the greatest performers to ever play come on and perform another familiar song of mine. It is such a treat to hear my songs the way I always heard them in my mind. Anyone who has ever tried to be a songwriter knows exactly what this night is all about. It has nothing to do with fame and fortune. It's all about hearing your songs performed with passion by people who get what you are saying and seeing the people listening to it embrace it and appreciate the creative talents that brought it to the stage that evening.

An incredible evening.

After the show, the family tree goes across the street and we all take over a nice bar there. I make the rounds, talking to everyone and hearing all the people in my family telling me how much they enjoyed this evening.

One by one, the family starts to empty the bar and head back to wherever they came from. Finally, it was me, Hermes, Mom, Dad and Grandpa sitting at a table.

"You know kid, there's more where that came from. The three of us are already working on one of those plays you wrote." Grandpa turns to

Hermes. "Where did you want to put that one on?"

"London. They have a grand theater there that would be just great."

"Yeah, that's right. Your Dad is coordinating everything so it should be another great evening."

"Maybe we could all work on some of your plays?" I toss out to Grandpa.

"Sure, kid. We have eternity after all. It will be fun for all of us to work together" He pauses, takes a sip from his drink and smiles. "You know, our family will certainly be well entertained with us over on this side, but I can't help but think – what the hell do people do for eternity when their family tree is full of plumbers?"

We all nearly fall out of our chairs in laughter. His point is well taken, though.

It's been a great evening, but it's time to rest. I say goodbye to Mom, Dad, Grandpa and Hermes and head back to my room.

I am stopped by Hermes. "Hey Andy, your Mom, Dad, Granny Dot, Panos, Ditty, Chuck and I are planning a trip to the Panagiotopulos estate in Greece. You want us to include you?"

I turn to Hermes. "You better. I would love to see that."

With that I'm back in my room. I decide to go into the Resource Center to relax and maybe check a few things out. Chris is already sitting at one of the tables reading through a few books.

"Hey Andy. How did your day go?"

I told him everything. Breakfast with Jesus, the concert with all my songs and the enjoyable time in the bar with the family tree.

"You know Chris, Grandpa made a comment that we all laughed at but I'm got me wondering. What DO people do when their family tree is full of plumbers?"

Chris laughs. "Well you don't bring your JOB over to this side Andy, you bring your passion. We don't have any pipes on this side that need fixing, ya know. Your passion is creative writing and it just happens to be the passion of many in your family. Some people have a real passion for camping or exploring the wilderness. Some have a passion for many other things. Your passions are passed on from generation to generation. That's by design so that when you come through the wash, your family has similar passions to work with."

It certainly makes sense to me. I'm really happy that my family has so much passion for entertainment. We can fill a lot of eternity with some pretty cool shows, I'm thinking.

After talking with Chris, I realize that I really am kind of beat. Instead of doing any research tonight, I'm thinking I'll just head back to my room and rest. It's been a long day, but a truly wonderful day.

"Listen Chris, I was thinking I might start my day tomorrow here in the Resource Center. Jesus gave me some names of some planets that I might find interesting and I thought I might check them out and plan out my day from that."

"Sounds good Andy. I know right where to go and I think you'll be surprised at what you can find. You did well today. You seem to be getting a hang of this side pretty good."

"Yeah, I'm getting more comfortable with it. I think you just have to realize that time doesn't apply on this side. I'm slowly learning to take my time with these fantasies and let them really develop and go their course without being anxious to move to another one."

"It's the hardest thing to adjust to on this side," says Chris in agreement.

"Oh hey Chris, how did Rosemary's tooth episode work out?"

"Great! Your day with her at the zoo really

helped her out. She went home from the dentists and decided that she was going to stop worrying about finances. She realizes that happiness comes from relationships and not bank accounts."

"That's my girl! How are the others doing?"

"They're fine. They miss you – but then you're such a miss-able kinda guy you know."

I smile, "I miss them, too". But for now, I'm going to catch some rest. It's been a great day.

With that, I get back to my bed and lay down. I think about breakfast with Jesus, the Savior of all mankind and the concert with my family and how my songs really came to life. I am so appreciative of my family and the love I continue to feel with every experience on this side. I'm also appreciative that these pillows are designed the way they are. It would be impossible to get to sleep tonight without them.

I'm starting to think Heaven is going to be a pretty nice way to spend eternity.

7

My Sixth Day

I wake up to day six. I have had some wonderful experiences and can see that with every experience, I am coming up with so many more ideas of how to spend a day here in eternity.

But today, I'm thinking I want to start out in the Resource Center. I'm thinking it would be nice to walk around and really see what that place is all about to help me better in the future.

I check my messages and there are none, so I go out the door that leads to the Resource Center and see Chris sitting at one of the tables browsing through a book. He probably knows what I was going to do before I did and that's starting to annoy me a bit – even though annoyance supposedly didn't come through the wash, but Guardian Angels sure to challenge that notion.

Chris notices me. "Hey Andy, how you doing today?"

"Well Chris, I thought I'd spend the day here in the Resource Center to get familiar with it and maybe check out a few places Jesus told me about."

"Good idea. Sit down and let me give you an overview and then I can show you around."

I sit down reluctantly as I am learning that arguing with Chris is not going to get me anywhere, even though I was kind of looking forward to browsing and discovering this place alone. But maybe an overview might be good.

"First, this Resource Center is your families Resource Center. Every family tree has their own Resource Center. It's especially designed for your family, utilizing all the interests and passions that are inherent in your family history. From generation to generation, your Resource Center has been growing. Every time a member of your family comes through the wash, this Resource Center grows up to the date of your passing."

I look a bit confused.

"Okay. You remember how I told you that your grandfather, Panos, could not go beyond his day of passing at 25 years?"

I nod, now even more confused. "Yeah."

"What I meant was that he could not create any fantasy that would have him older than 25 years because there is no reality that registers him beyond his 25th year. He will always have fantasies within the 25 years of reality registered. However, every time a family member passes through the wash, that day becomes the new 'up to' day from which fantasies can occur for any member of your family tree. That's one reason why everyone is so happy to see you. They now have a whole new block of time that they can explore and develop their fantasies from."

"So you're saying Panos, because I'm here, can now go to New York City in the year 2032, but he has to be 25 years old or younger?"

"Exactly! All the books here at the Resource Center became updated to 2032 on the day you came through the wash, not to mention all the new additions of your personal writings that were added on that day as well. And as you learned on your first day, you retain everything on this side because it all comes from love. So, while you were getting indoctrinated with me, all your family members were here in the Resource Center getting all the updates."

"But I came through here and I didn't see anybody. In fact, every time I come here the place is empty."

"That's right. The Resource Center is a place for you to come and research whatever you want. You must be able to do so without a lot of distractions. So every time you come here, it will be empty, unless it's written on your paper that you want a non-fantasy day at the Resource Center with whoever's name you put at the top of the paper."

"So Panos, who came here in the early 1920s, now can completely understand how computers work and how people can get from Paris to New York in a matter of hours?"

"Absolutely. But it comes gradually. Your family members who lived during the time of Jesus now understand how computers work too, but they have been gradually learning how all these things have evolved as every passing generation has come through the wash. It's never overwhelming and actually becomes an exciting way to spend a day. This Resource

Center really gets a lot of use – especially when a new family member comes through the wash."

I'm fascinated by all this but as I think about it, it makes a lot of sense. I'm not inclined to challenge any of this with more questions because I'd rather get up and start exploring this place on my own. I start to get up.

"Well thanks Chris, that really helps out. I think I'll just brows around and kind of get a feel for this place for a bit."

"Okay, I'll leave you be." says Chris. "But before I do, let me point out a few things" He gets up and stands by me. "As you can see, the topic is clearly marked. Over there is science. Over there's history. And over there is music. You can figure that out I'm sure. Now in front of every section, there is a stand that just has a flat square on it. Do you see it over there at the science section?"

I look closer and sure enough there is a stand that looks somewhat like a music stand but is just flat and inconspicuous. "Yeah, I see it."

"They have one of those at every topic. They are called the Finders. They are connected to everything in that topic. Now, let's say you want to look up those planets Jesus was telling you about."

I nod enthusiastically. "Okay."

"You would put one hand over your heart and the other hand on the Finder and the desire of your heart would connect with the Finder and the best book for you would automatically start blinking so you can find it."

"Get outta here. That's all I have to do? How cool is that? That's way better than having to figure out all the codes on a library card."

"It is nice, but be careful. You really need to be specific before you connect your heart to the Finder. In this case you would concentrate. I want to check out the planets that Jesus was telling me about. Concentrate. Hand on your heart, the other on the Finder. Bingo – the book you need is blinking until you get it. Or you can ask a question. I'd like to check out the best planets to go surfing. Hand over your heart, other on the Finder. There it is. The best planets to go surfing blinking away."

"Wow, this is going to be fun." I pause. "But why did you say to be careful? There's more to it, right?"

"Well you have to be concentrating on what you want to find before you put your hand on the Finder. If you start to wander away from what you're looking for as you put your hand on the Finder, it will be confused and smack you."

"Smack me?"

"Oh, yes. It's not very pleasant. If the information is unclear, the Finder sends it back to you with a nasty dose of current to smack you back into concentrating. It usually happens when a few people are here planning future fantasies. One will cover their heart and then start talking to the other as they put their other hand on the Finder, and smack! Boy, those people jump when that happens. But in most cases, it only happens to a person once before they learn to stay focused when standing near the Finders.

"Now over here is where I showed you all your books, plays and scripts, remember?"

"Yeah. I'm definitely going to spend some time in that area."

"You sure will, because I didn't tell you that's your family room. All your Grandfathers works, Carlton Smith. It is filled with your relatives writing. There's even a section of your Dad's scripts."

"Dad's scripts?"

"Sure. Your Dad always wanted to write scripts for movies. Don't you remember all those times you talked to him and he was giving you ideas for stories? Your dad had a most creative mind and even though it never materialized back on Earth, those ideas became scripts over here and are yours to enjoy."

"How cool is that! I always thought he should have been a writer. Alright, Pops!"

"And here's the nice thing, Andy. You can get one of your Dad's script, read through it, and if you want, just go over to that door over there and step inside and you'll be able to sit down and watch the full movie just as it should have been filmed. Come back, get one of your Grandpa's plays, go back through that door and watch the play the way it was meant to be. You have eternity, so you can spend a day here watching a whole lot of movies and plays. Your family has so many forms of entertainment in this room, you'll be thankful that God gives you that eternity. Gosh, you remember all those songs you wrote and how you envisioned the music videos for them? Take your songs with you into that room and see exactly how each video would have been."

"Wow! Oh, this IS SO Heaven, Chris. I hardly know where to begin with all this. Man, the ideas are flying through my mind and I don't know how to start."

"Just remember Andy, time has no value here. Why not start with those planets Jesus was telling you about?"

"You're right, Chris. But I might need a lot of paper and pencils to write down everything."

"No you won't. Remember when you worked on computers on the other side? Every time you came to a web site that you really liked, you just saved it in your favorites."

I am wigging out with excitement. "Yeah, can I do that over here?"

"Sure. Our system is even better. As you're going through a book and see something that you'd like to save, just point to it, put your hand over your heart and say, 'save' and it's saved for you. Over there by your family room. You see that big thing that looks like a Finder?"

"Yeah."

'It's like a Finder only it sets up your favorites. When you are done, you go over to your Favorites Finder and there is a keyboard. Push any key and a screen pops up on the surface. It asks you what topic. You point to science. It pulls up all the saves from that section. You point to the planet Jesus told you about and it pulls up everything you wanted saved about it. You can even plan out a fantasy on it if you want. You can fill in the names you want at the top, complete the sentence, 'Today I am going to___' and then just save it to your fantasy file. Any day you're not sure what you want to do, just come in here and look in your fantasy file and you can print out any one you want."

"How cool is that?"

"Very cool. And you can even look up stuff before you go to the Finders. You just point to the search button. Put your hand over your heart and other hand on the screen, then concentrate on the place you saw on TV a long time ago that looked like a fun place to go. As your thinking about it, a picture will pop up on the screen. If it's what you're thinking of, you point to yes and it gives you all the info you need. Then you go over to the Finder in the Destinations section and you know exactly what you want it to find for you. It really cuts back on the smacking to be sure."

"Thanks, Chris. I'm sure there are a million questions and things to learn here, but I think I'll head over to check out some Jesus planets and get a feel for this place."

"I'll leave you be. There is a lot more to this

place for sure. Some I' know sure you'll figure out on your own, but if you ever have any questions, you know where to find me."

With that, Chris heads back to his room and leaves me to my exploration.

Boy, I never imagined that the Resource Center would be that fascinating. I'm thinking this is going to be one of my longest days ever by the time I get through here. But then again, Chris keeps reminding me how time has no place on this side. I don't have to explore everything at once. I'm thinking I'll go over to the science area and look up those planets that Jesus told me about. After all, he is the Savior of all mankind and he did make the suggestion. It would really be uncool if I spent a lot of time watching Dad's movies before I finally got around to Jesus, the Savior of all mankind, planets. I'm sure Dad would understand that reasoning, so I'm off to the science area.

I stand and stare at the Finder. Somehow I have the feeling that it's going to smack me the first time just to mock me. You can never trust anyone connected to the science field, you know. I concentrate. I want to check out the planets that Jesus, the Savior of all mankind told me to, please. I put my hand over my heart, then

I extend my hand towards the surface of the Finder. I want to check out the planets that Jesus, the Savior of all mankind told me to, please. My eyes closed, I touch the surface of the Finder and quickly jump out of the way. I slowly open my eyes and look around. Nothing. Suddenly, I notice in the distance a blinking light. I perk up. I start towards the blinking light, stepping very wide, as far away from the Finder, that I still don't trust. As I get to the blinking light, I notice it is not a blinking light but a blinking book.

"Cool!"

I take the book from the shelf. The Two Planets That Jesus, Savior of All Mankind, Thinks Andy Smith Might Like To Visit. Good title. I take the book and find a seat at the table. Chris is back in his office and I truly have the place to myself.

I start reading through my book. Wow. The first planet is named Gurtz and seems to be full of nature. It's like a planet with nothing but Yellowstone Park on it. Lots of animals, some I'm familiar with, others I have never seen before. Pages of mountains with snow and deserts with playful dunes. Beautiful beaches and valleys. Beautiful scenery that seems endless. There doesn't appear to be any man-made stuff. No cities, cars, planes. Just nature. But I did find a huge hotel nestled in the middle of it all. Wow. What a great get away place for a family reunion, I think. I put my hand over my heart and point to the picture of this hotel and say – Save – and continue on. I stop at the ocean pictures and notice the same hotel sitting by the beaches. Hmmm. I think I'm picking up on the idea here. Maybe these books are written by your heart and are just there to show you the possibilities as you plan your fantasies.

Well Gurtz was interesting and frankly quite obviously being that it was recommended by Jesus, the Savior of all mankind after all. I flip the page and come to my second planet, Bork.

Now Bork is kind of an odd place. There are all kinds of creatures busily going about. The pictures seem like a scene out of Star Wars or something. Lots of weird creatures, buildings and activity. I'm curious after Gurtz, why Jesus would recommend this one.

I start reading some of the captions and as I do I start to become quite attracted to the place. It seems that with all these different creatures, the only common thread between them is, what I'm being told, a wonderful sense of humor. A

Planet that specializes in a great sense of humor between all species of animals. Well I've always been a sucker for people with a good sense of humor. And frankly, I'm tickled to think that this planet would be one of the first ones recommended to me by Jesus, the Savior of all mankind! But after my breakfast with him, I'm not completely surprised. You don't become the Savior of all mankind without a pretty healthy sense of humor, I'm thinking.

This is great. And the last part of the book gives brief samples of many other planets out there under the heading of, 'If you think Gurtz and Bork are cool, you're going to also like' And sure enough, I'm anxious to check many of them out as well.

But for now, I'm feeling a bit run out of gas. I'm thinking I've got enough information to encourage me to make the Resource Center a standard stop in my eternity planning.

As I head back to my room, I'm thinking about all the possible fantasies I could have on Gurtz alone. And Bork. And all the plays, movies, music videos and possibilities that exists just in my own family room.

As I get to my door, I hear a snapping pop that shakes me as I bolt around to see what happened. I look around and am still alone. Then it occurs to me. I'm betting Dad, Hermes and Grandpa are planning something else and they just got a bit carried away with their talking while standing at a Finder.

I start to laugh as I head to my bed. I'm thinking my Family Tree Resource Center probably has the highest electric bill in all eternity.

God I love this place.

8

My Seventh Day

After all that has happened to me this past six days, I wake up this morning thinking today I'm going to have a day off. I've learned so much in every adventure and I really feel the need to take a break and simply enjoy a day to myself. Of course, it's not hard to guess where that will be. I'm going to spend my day surfing on a nice beach in Hawaii!

I get up and am happy to see no blinking messages. I take my sheet and simply write, Today, I'm going to spend the day surfing on a beautiful beach in Hawaii.'

I head to the door, open it and am standing before the most beautiful sight – next to my girls – I've ever seen. It's a gorgeous day with the sun peeking up from the Pacific blue waters. I go and find my lounge chair nicely laid out with a beach blanket laying over it. Next to the lounge is the perfect surfboard for me. The right size and width for my tastes. Behind the surfboard is a beautiful resort and a outside bar that I am certain will keep those umbrella drinks coming.

I stand there taking it all in. I think of how God made all the Heavens and the Earth in six days and on the seventh day he rested. Let there be no doubt that this is exactly where God would want to spend that seventh day!

I look out at the ocean. The waves are perfect. There seems to be little wind spray and I see no signs of any rip currents. The waves seem to be yelling at me, "Can Andy come out and play?!" I smile and without hesitating, I grab my surfboard and head for the ocean where I spend a great time conquering the mighty waves one by one.

I realize that Chris was right – there are no consequences on this side. Even when I wipe out, I come up laughing and enjoying every moment of being tossed about by the victorious wave. I could do this forever, but for now, I'm thinking I want to go back in and simply lay around for a while with an umbrella drink or two.

As I lay on the beach lounge with my umbrella drink, I start to go over everything that I have learned this week. Coming through the wash to get all the negative gunk out of my heart. The family reunion and meeting all those wonderful people that I can now call family. Speaking Latin to my girls and learning how things work when you are with people from 'the other side'. Spending the day at grandpas on W45th street in New York City. The walks along the beaches. My day at the Zoo with Rosemary who was having a tooth pulled. The talks with Chris. The breakfast with Jesus, the Savior of all mankind who likes his eggs sunny side up and the many stories to discover in my PIP book. The concert with my family and all my songs and the drinks afterwards at the bar. The day spent exploring and learning all the great things about the Resource Center.

Boy, this has been a great week. When you're living on Earth, you always wonder how Heaven will be. Will you recognize others there? Will you remember your life on Earth? Will you be able to influence those you left behind? How can you find happiness in Heaven and have it still make sense?

I now have the answers to those questions, and though I am certain that there are many other questions that may come up after my first week in eternity, I'm beginning to see how this really can work.

It's amazing really, how much it makes sense. You only live on Earth for a short while, but its just enough time to put your heart of love through all the emotional cycles of living in a world of consequences and free wills. This is what builds the true foundation of a heart. When you come through the wash, all that negative stuff gets washed away and the love in your heart has all the character and strength that was developed in that imperfect world. And now you have an eternity to build on that foundation of love through all your fantasies created from the roots of love.

I'm thinking this is going to be a great eternity for me. I start to think of what I would like to do next. I have so many fantasies that I want to pursue. So many family members from generations past I want to spend time with. The girls, of course. I have some trips to far away galaxies to explore and that's with only ONE book out of the Resource Center so far! I want so bad to work with Dad, Grandpa and Hermes and explore all the creative possibilities that our hearts can create.

I'm beginning to think too much. I decide to just close my eyes and take in the beauty of the moment. I listen to the gentle crashing of the waves and take a sip from my delicious umbrella drink as I begin to empty out my thoughts and simply relax.

Meanwhile, back at the Resource Center, Chris is relaxing in his office flipping through the pages of another book when another Angel comes through the door. Chris looks up and smiles right away. He recognizes her.

"I was hoping you'd drop by soon. How are things going?"

"She came through the wash yesterday. She's with her Family Tree right now."

"How's she doing?"

"Great. She's got a strong heart and she was totally amazed when I explained everything to her."

Chris hesitates, "Did she ask about him?"

The Angel smiles even wider. "Oh, yeah. Once she learned how this all works it was the first thing she asked about."

Chris perks up. "Excellent! What did you tell her?"

"I smiled and said, 'Welcome to Heaven' and that it could be better than she ever imagined. Of course, she quickly changed the subject and started asking about other stuff, but I could see it in her eyes." The Angel pauses, "Do you think we should do it?"

Chris doesn't give the question much thought. "Are you kidding?! We have an obligation to do it!"

"Well, okay. Where is he now?"

"He's on a beach in Hawaii. It would be perfect."

"Are you sure he'll be ok with it?"

"Are you kidding me? He's been avoiding that fantasy since he got here. If we don't force the issue with him, he'll never get around to it on his own. Trust me, He's going to be ok with this one."

They both smile. The Angel gets the right settings from Chris and heads out the door. Chris sits back in his chair with a grin so wide and warm you sense he is about to explode with celebration.

Back at the beach, I'm embracing my day off the way it should be embraced. I'm in no hurry to do anything. I just want to lay with my eyes closed and my umbrella drink close by and soak in every feature of this beautiful setting.

"Mind if I join you?"

I freeze.

My heart stops and soars at the same time.

I know that voice without opening my eyes. And it's saying the words I have wanted to hear for so long.

All I can do is smile like I have never smiled before.

Now there is no doubt that I truly am in Heaven.

9

The End

(So, what are your 1st seven days going to be like?)

BUT WAIT

THERE'S MORE!

10

Note To Readers

Please understand that from this point on, any future 'days in heaven' will not be put in chronological order as there is NO time in heaven, so there actually are NO days in heaven. When I put a day on future days, it's not really THAT day because there are NO days, just a bunch of fantasies being lived out to help fuel the love God needs. If this is a problem for you and you become frantic because there's a day eleven but where is day nine, or day ten?, I will send Chris down to get you straightened out. He's proven pretty good at dealing with idiots.

Andy Smith

The Author

11

My Eighth Day

This eternity thing has really been exciting and clearly the hardest part is trying to keep your mind from exploding. Your mind is constantly racing at 100 miles per hour thinking of the many ways you can spend a day. You have to constantly remind yourself that there is no time frame on this side. Eventually, I'll learn to relax and just go with my impulse when I get up every day, knowing that whatever I choose to do can go as long as I want it to go without affecting any of my future fantasies. But with my creative mind going crazy with a constant flow of ideas for fantasies, I'm guessing that this is easier said than done. At least in my case.

There is one part of all this that has been troubling me though. I understand that when I came to this side I went through the wash and only the love came through. That's fine and makes sense, I suppose, but I can't help but think that many of our successes in the past are magnified because of the struggles and disappointments that preceded it. As a writer on the other side, I remember those few moments when I had success that the celebration wasn't just in finally getting something published, but more that I persevered through all the rejections and disappointments and didn't give up. That was as much the celebration as the actual story being published.

If only the positives get through the wash, how can our successes ever be as meaningful or satisfying on this side if there are no references to the feelings of struggles and disappointments that lead up to that success?

I'm sure I'll figure this all out in time and I am certainly confident that God knows what He is doing on this side. I'm not the first one to come through the wash after all, and I'm not the kind of guy with an ego that would suggest that I have found a flaw in Gods system. If I've learned anything these past seven days, it's that I don't know squat about how things work on this side, and it would be wise for me to just keep quiet about it and trust that the answer will come in due time.

So today I'm thinking I might spend some time in the Resource Center and develop some solid ideas for future fantasies I want to pursue. After all, it's not like I don't already have a million ideas flashing through my mind, so why not throw some more logs on that fire and see if I might well be the first person to go completely insane in Heaven.

I check the message machine – no messages – and head out to the Resource Center, where- of course- I find Chris sitting at the table browsing through a book he probably doesn't need to read because he already knows everything. I know he's been a great help to me in understanding how things work on this side, but I've always been a guy who likes to explore things on my own. Sometimes I think the adventure can get lost if everything is simply explained to you before you have a chance to explore it.

I look over and just like that Chris disappears.

I panic! I just killed my Guardian Angel by thinking!!

Holy Cow!!!

I nervously go over to his office and open the door, only to find Chris quietly sitting there reading the same book. He looks up at me and smiles.

"How did you do that?" I ask, trying to catch my breath.

His smile turns into that familiar look that tells me without words that my question doesn't warrant any response from him.

"I thought you had some questions, but apparently, you want to be left alone" He says with an innocent smile.

One of the hardest things for me to get use to is the creepy way Chris knows everything I am thinking. It annoys me to no end as I am also reminded that this is going to go on for eternity, and with only the positive stuff getting through the wash, I'm a tad bit pissed off that I may well lose my membership on this side and get thrown back through the wash with all the homicidal thoughts this creepy little angel keeps generating in my mind.

"Relax Andy. Remember, this is your eternity, not mine. Certainly I know what you are thinking, but my role is never to judge, but to serve as a guide for you. To answer any questions you might have on this side and how it all works. In many ways, I'm just like this book. You're only going to find me in the Resource Center because that's all I really am – a resource for you just as this book is. I am full of information that can guide you and help you develop the eternity that best suits your heart. The only difference between me and this book is that I can talk to you and help you with suggestions based on my understanding of how you think and feel. You need to stop looking at me as a threat and start thinking of me as a valuable resource for you as you plan your eternity. I have no authority to throw you back through the wash. I'm simply here to help."

There is absolutely nothing worse than talking to someone who can innocently turn your homicidal thoughts into guilt!

"Well that's just great. Once again you've managed to gently turn my thoughts of contempt for you into guilt. You make it really hard to feel the love that supposedly was the only thing that came through the wash, you know!"

Chris smiles and gestures to me to sit down

with eyes that tell me to shut up and take a deep breath. I brace myself for what I've come to expect to be a generous piece of humble pie as I take my seat.

"Andy, you're doing fine. You just have to give God more credit. You're not the first person to come through the wash, ya know. It takes time to get the hang of this place, for sure. There are a lot of questions and anxiety in the challenges of creating your own Heaven. It's an emotional roller-coaster for many people for a bit. God doesn't expect people to get it right away. He understands that until a person fully grasps the possibilities of this side and the resources available, there is bound to be feelings of frustration and uncertainty, and in your case, homicidal thoughts I suppose. It's all good Andy. Nobody is going to throw you back through the wash. You've earned your eternity and once you get all these initial questions and concerns worked out, I have no doubt that your eternity is going to be a very positive, fulfilling experience for you."

I pause and swallow my humble pie and let what Chris has said sink in. Once again I realize that maybe I've been too hard on Chris and maybe he is right that I should look at him as a resource instead of a threat.

"Sorry Chris. I guess a guy like me just takes longer to figure stuff like this out."

"Don't be so hard on yourself. God likes your type. You have a very loving heart that certainly got you through the wash fairly easily. And you have such a rebellious spirit that challenges everything. That's a great combination because God knows that once someone like you figures it out and begins to tap into the many possibilities of this new world, your eternity is going to be one great adventure after another. I am in no way offended by your thoughts of homicide towards me," his smile nearly breaks into laughter, "And I assure you that once you do get the hang of this place, you'll be seeing less and less of me as you develop your future adventures. I truly am just a resource for you here."

He pauses to let me take this all in before he continues.

"I was sitting out in the Resource Center because I thought you had some questions about feelings of how successes on this side might not be as rewarding because there are no failures, which is a great question that I wanted to help you with."

"Well you did say that nobody gets hurt on this side. Sometimes those hurts and disappointments are what makes our successes so much more gratifying."

"You are absolutely right to question that, Andy. Certainly, receiving a check for $300 bucks for an article isn't nearly as exciting unless you include the backdrop of all the rejections and disappointments that came before it. That makes perfect sense. But remember when you came through the wash and the Guardian of the Book of Life told you that only the memories that had a positive outcome came through the wash? The outcome is the key here. Everything on this side must have a positive outcome. Certainly, many of our positive outcomes came at a great expense to our hearts. It's those struggles, rejections and disappointments that builds character and without a strong character, those positive outcomes can be very shallow and meaningless. Your eternity is going to be very superficial without the struggles and disappointments that built the character you needed to bring you to your successes. All those feelings and emotions are needed to contribute to a more impactful, positive outcome. The positive outcome is what's important here, but the road that brought that positive outcome is just as valuable."

I'm sitting up now and feeling much more positive about what Chris is saying. Once again, it totally makes sense and I'm actually feeling a little grateful that Chris can read my mind as I would have likely wasted half my eternity trying to figure this out without ever coming up with this answer. And of course, Chris has again shown his mastery at turning my annoyance at him and directed it back at me as I hear that little voice of conscience quietly whispering, "you're an idiot".

"Remember Andy, to think of me as a resource for you, just like this book. Only my information is all about your life. Let me give you an example of what I can do for you.

"Say you wanted to spend a day capturing your success as a writer, but you are not sure what or where you want that fantasy to be. Remember, I have complete reference to everything you did in your past life. I can pinpoint every emotion you ever had and can direct you to the exact moment those feelings filled your heart. You can come to me and say, 'Chris, I want to experience the feeling of success as a writer but have no idea where to begin.' I will know exactly what your are feeling and give you a number. You can go over to the Favorites Finder I told you about here in the Resource Center and enter that number. It will pull up a number of pictures from your life with short captions for you to choose from. Each picture represents a specific time in your life that you may or may not remember that could have been a real turning point for you as a writer but for whatever reason, did not turn out so well. When you select the one you want, you can save it into your Fantasy Favorites file for a future use, or select, 'Play it Now', and go through the door I showed you and watch the story unfold as you wish. Your heart will dictate the fantasy and it can go as long as you wish it to go. It can be a short fantasy that just gives you that one moment of success, or you can create a lifetime from that experience that creates more successes as a writer. It's your fantasy. That's why I am here, Andy. You had so many fantasies in your life and there is really no way that you could remember them all. I can direct you to every feeling you ever had and give you the opportunity to create a great fantasy with a positive outcome. It's just one more tool you have to create your eternity into an exciting and positive Heaven."

Wow, this is so cool. The opportunity to go back and rewrite those many rejections I had as a writer and turn them into a positive outcome is really exciting to think about. Once again, I'm reminded of why God made this side eternal. It's hard to wrap your mind around all the possibilities and with each new discovery, you really appreciate the fact that there is no time limit in creating your own Heaven.

I get up as I'm anxious to get back to the Resource Center to explore, when I pause and turn to Chris.

"What's in it for God? I mean, this is all really cool stuff and all for me, but it truly creates a really selfish world for me. What does God get out of me living out all my fantasies like this?"

"Are you kidding? God is Love. You are creating the fuel that makes love strong. Every person who comes through the wash adds to the strength of the love that feeds God. With each fantasy you create, God's love grows stronger. Every time someone carries out another fantasy, God's love grows stronger. God realized at the beginning that for love to be universal and pure, it also had to be selfish. You are just starting your eternity. Many of the fantasies you create now may appear to be self-centered. As you go along and understand the possibilities this new world of yours has, your fantasies will become more powerful in the love it creates, which helps God become stronger. Pure love always starts out selfish, but grows into a powerful, universal love that God needs to survive. You – and everyone else who comes through the wash- are a vital part of God's plan. God is Love, and you living out your fantasies are an important reason why that love remains so strong."

Double Wow! I am truly humbled by this answer Chris has given me. For the first time, I feel as if I truly am an important part of Heaven. I am so motivated to create great fantasies that will strengthen God's love. I'm excited at the thought that my fantasies here in my own selfish little eternity is going to contribute to the hope of all those still living in my past world.

God IS love, and I finally am realizing that I have an important role in keeping that love strong.

WOW! That's some pretty powerful thinking there, but I'm beginning to feel as if I really do get it.

As I start out the door, Chris finishes up,

"You're doing a great job, Andy. I'm here if you need anything. And by the way. No matter how annoying I may be, you'll never be able to kill me. I'm an angel, remember?"

I can do without that smirk on his face and am not all that comfortable with his comment.

12

My Eleventh Day

When I get out of my restful slumber, I'm thinking I might just head into the Resource Center and look around. I'm not sure what exactly I want to do next and with time not being a factor on this side, I don't feel any sense of urgency to check another fantasy off my bucket list.

As I go through the door, I notice Chris sitting at a table looking through a book. I'm not bothered by his presence, but I've been on this side long enough to know Chris would not be sitting there unless he knew something that I don't know and whether I like it or not, I'm going to hear about something new.

"How's it going, Chris?"

"Couldn't be better. You?"

"Great, thanks. Thought I'd take a break from all these fantasies and spend a little time here in the Resource Center."

"Good idea. There's plenty to draw from in here that's for sure."

"So Chris, now that I'm on this side and have figured out all this fantasy living stuff, I'm guessing you don't have much to do any more but read books, right?"

Chris laughs out loud. "Oh no. We Guardian Angels have a lot of work to do. Networking with each other and making sure everything is going in a positive direction. There's plenty for me to do."

I was afraid he would say something like that. Now I know I'd be well advised to take a seat and cut to the chase. "So with so much to do, I'm guessing you're sitting here reading a book because there is something I have missed or done wrong that you need to tell me about?"

"No, not at all, Andy. You're doing a great job and I love the way you have adjusted to your new world. I'm just here because you were not sure what direction you wanted to go next, and I thought I'd make myself available to maybe give you some suggestions or new ideas that maybe you haven't thought of."

I'm afraid to ask. "So there's more than what you have already told me?"

Chris laughs again. "Oh my yes! There are many more opportunities to fulfill your fantasies on this side. That's why God made time irrelevant over here. You think you can fill up eternity with what I have given you, yet the truth is that I have only given you a fraction of the possibilities so far."

I stare at Chris as someone delivers a rather refreshing looking beverage to me, which I did NOT ask for but I'm certain that my guardian angel, who knows everything to an annoyance about me and knows that I might need a drink ordered it, and truth be told, I'm thinking a strong drink just might hit the spot if this guy keeps talking, so I take a sip and sure enough, this is one awesome drink, which again concerns me because if what he has to share with me requires this kind of awesomeness, I might be in for an uncomfortable ride here.

"Well since you already got me this swell

drink, I might as well listen to your ideas. What do you have for me now?"

Chris laughs. "I delight in your lack of trust in me. It's really quite charming."

"And I delight in how I always end up with my foot in my mouth and having to apologize to you for my dire lack of faith, so go ahead and charm me with your new ideas."

Chris really does seem to delight in our conversations, and you'd think by now I'd have learned to understand that everything he has to say is truly in my best interest and I shouldn't be so skeptical around him. That being said, this is a new world I'm in and I guess I just get nervous and afraid of messing all this goodness up. His positive perkiness can be rather annoying under the circumstances I would say.

"Well Andy, I was just thinking that you'd be an excellent candidate for our Heart Program."

"Heart Program? What the hell is that? I thought you said I could eat whatever I wanted on this side. Now you're going to get me into some health and fitness program?"

Chris nearly falls out of his chair in laughter and of course, I'm a bit offended that he finds this so funny.

"No, no, no. It's not a fitness program. This

is a program where people like you on this side can become the conscience of someone down on Earth and help them to make positive decisions in their life and keep them going in the right direction."

I again stare at Chris with a pained look on my face as I take another sip of my drink. I have no idea what he is talking about, but I'm sure I'll find out if I just listen.

"Okayyy ..... go on?"

"Well, let's see. Remember how you wanted to be a baseball player when you were growing up?"

"I do." I say cautiously.

"Well I have many young men down on your Earth who have tons of baseball talent and are closing in on a crossroad in their life. I could assign one to you and you could become his conscience. You would experience all the joys of being a big league baseball player through him and he would benefit from you being his conscience and drawing from all the life experiences you had when you were there."

"So you want me to take over this kids life?"

"No, no, no. You don't take over his life, you simply become his conscience. You know how you use to tell your girls to follow their heart?"

"Yes."

"And you hear people say to listen to your conscience, follow your heart, follow your best instincts. What do you think your conscience is?"

"ummmmmm ... I have no idea, but I'm sure you'll fill me in?"

"With the Heart Program on this side, we have many people who sign up to become the conscience of someone we – me and the other Guardian Angels- feel is a good match for and they can use their experiences to become the conscience of people on Earth and help them have positive outcomes in their life."

"Isn't that cheating?"

"No. Of course not! It's not a competition, it's life. The ultimate goal is to get everyone through the wash, right?"

"Yeeeeaaaa..... but....."

"Oh Andy, you're thinking too much like a human."

"Well that's where my experience is ya know."

"I know, I know, but think of it this way. God is Love, right?"

"Ooooooooookkkkkay...."

"And love is not a physical object, it's a spirit, an emotion. Your body didn't come through the wash, the love in your heart came through the wash. You can use that love to create your own heaven and in doing so, you do your part to make the love in heaven ever stronger. And God is love, so by living out your fantasies, you are making God stronger."

"Ooooooookkkkkk .... I get that, but...."

"On the other side, down on Earth, people have a conscience. That voice in their head that tells them what direction to go, right?"

"Yea, well that voice in my head said I was an idiot more than a few times, ya know!"

"Well it can be frustrating work, but I think if you go back to those times you'll see that she wasn't technically incorrect in her assessment."

"I had a GIRL for a conscience!?!"

"Andy, Andy, Andy! Once again, you are thinking physical when you need to start thinking spiritual. A doctor down there can not operate on a person to fix their conscience like they do a broken arm. It is a spiritual thing, not a physical thing."

"But you had a woman in my head calling me an idiot? No wonder I threw away my cleats and quit baseball!"

Chris bows his head and shakes it in utter anguish. "Andy, stay with me here. Trust me. Once you understand how this all works, it will make total sense to you, I assure you. Well, at least I hope so."

"Well you're the one trying to sell me this Heart Program which isn't a fitness program but a head job where I can experience my fantasy of being a baseball player while telling this kid to stay away from the PEDs, and that sounds cool. But then you casually mention that MY conscience was a GIRL, so what am I to think? How do I know that if I sign up for this, you won't be sticking me inside the head of some Opera singer with instructions to guide her towards a loving world, when I'd rather be telling her, 'Honey, lose a hundred pounds and become a hooker so I can get out of this God forsaken opera world!'"

Chris glares at me as he tries desperately to gather himself. He takes a deep breath and calmly continues.

"First of all, we have plenty of people on this side who truly appreciate Opera and would have no problem finding an appropriate conscience to work with a young lady and keep her from becoming a hooker."

I sit back in my chair a bit smug, but bracing myself for more. "Well, I was just say'n. You're not doing a very good job of selling this program to me. I mean, did my girly conscience want to experience being a baseball player?"

Chris continues to glare at me in a manner that makes me quite uncomfortable and frankly very un-Angel like. It is clear he will not be responding to my question.

"Secondly, you would have complete say in what assignment you take. We have plenty of opportunities down on Earth and we have plenty of people in the Heart Program who want to help. We have many on this side who spend all their time working in the Heart Program. When they are done with one assignment, they are ready to take on another. I have access to many who put no restrictions on the assignment. They've been doing it for a long time and fully understand the 'spirituality' of the assignment and how their work as a conscience truly helps to create more love."

My curiosity is perked. "You mean there are some on this side who never fill out one of those sheets? Don't they have any fantasies to fulfill?"

"You have to remember that everyone on this side is unique and their heaven is created from their uniqueness. Not everyone starts out with a family tree day like you did Some people have family histories that would never come through the wash. Others have spent so much time living on Earth in a life of service. Mother Teresa, many Priests, there are a lot of people, Andy, who come from a totally different experience than you have. Sure, some of them may give the fantasy sheets a try, but there are many who once they find out about the Heart Program and become a conscience for others down on Earth, they become hooked and have no desire to do anything else."

"So there are some who spend their whole eternity being a conscience in all kinds of people? What if the person doesn't work out? What if they stop listening to their heart?"

"The person always has the choice. God gave everyone a free will. The conscience only advises, but if the person doesn't listen to their heart, you would have the choice to abort the assignment entirely, or you could choose to stay with it a little longer and keep trying to get through."

"So if my baseball guy decides not to listen to me and goes for the PEDs, I can bail on him?"

"Yes. Or you can say 'You're an idiot' and hang with him and keep trying. Your choice"

Well I certainly don't like Chris's reference here, and I give him a look to let him know as I try to stay on subject. "So we give up on the guy? He doesn't have a conscience any more?"

"Everyone has a conscience. The Guardian Angels have a large pool of people on this side who want to participate in the Heart Program. If you feel you have reached a point where you need to abort, you should do so. You can take on another assignment, or maybe go back and try a few more fantasies. It's your choice. We will replace you with someone else the second you abort."

"But if I abort and you have to replace me with someone else on this side, wouldn't I feel like I failed?"

"Well you probably would, but you shouldn't. Remember, the ultimate objective is to advance love and help love grow. It doesn't matter who the conscience is, we are happy to have people on this side ready to help advance the love in everyone on Earth and get them through the wash. When you were on Earth, I had to use four different people – and yes, one of them was a woman in her earthly life- to work with you as your conscience."

"Is that a lot? Was I that difficult that people kept bailing on me?"

Chris again laughs out loud at my comment

that I think is perfectly reasonable, as a server delivers another of my awesome drinks as if Chris knew I needed one, which of course, I did!

"You are so competitive Andy. It doesn't matter. I would have gladly used a hundred people as your conscience if it meant getting you through the wash. Your work in the Heart Program will have no affect on your PIP number. It will have no affect on your position here in Heaven. It's your Heaven to create as you wish. Some people try the Heart Program and quickly learn that it's not their cup of tea. That's fine. The Heart Program is merely another opportunity we have for people on this side that they can use to create their unique Heaven with. Remember, you have to think spiritually now and not physically. The only goal here is to advance love and create environments that will strengthen and advance LOVE. If you want to focus on your fantasies, great. If you want to participate in the Heart Program, great. It doesn't matter to us. We just want to advance love. You decide how you can personally help us achieve that."

I take a sip from my delicious beverage as I thoughtfully stare at Chris. This Heart Program does have possibilities, but I'm not sure if I'm quite ready to take it on. Chris, of course, knows my hesitance as he gets up to leave.

"Think about it. I think you'd do great in the Heart Program, but you certainly don't need to decide right now. I just thought I'd present this program to you as you look for other opportunities here in the Resource Center. I'll leave alone."

As Chris is leaving, I acknowledge his help.

"Thanks for letting me know about it. But let me tell you, pal, if I decide to do this and you put me inside the head of a baseball player in the Dodgers organization, I swear I'll have him on PEDs in no time. I hate the Dodgers. Why, I'd rather be put in the head of that Opera singer!"

"I can arrange that!" He says laughingly as he goes into his office.

"Can I have another drink here, please!"

13

My Fifteenth Day

As I get up to start a new day and a new fantasy, I sit on my bed and think about it all. I'm really getting comfortable with my Heaven and am so impressed with how this all works and how much sense it makes. I laugh to myself at the thought that so many people on the other side think they have Heaven all figured out and the reality is they are not even close. It's no wonder that nobody on this side ever wants to go back to the other side. No clocks and no consequences. Just a world of living out fantasies every day without end.

As I'm simmering in my thoughts, I notice my message light is blinking. I reach over to see what's up. It's Chris.

"Hey Andy, I want to show you something in the Resource Center you might find interesting. Just come over."

I hesitate. I always do when Chris is involved. I know he's my guardian angel and he's been right every time I challenge him. Or he challenges me, I suppose. But I haven't reached that level of confidence in him yet that makes me get excited when he leaves me a message like this. He has a nasty knack for leaving out little details about this world that makes me speak Latin to my daughters and go ballistic when Rosemary has a tooth pulled. I just have that feeling that every time he wants to 'show me something', I'm in for a bumpy ride.

I go through the door and into the Resource Center and find Chris standing there with a big smile on his face. That smile annoys me so much because it almost always is followed by some bad news for me.

"Hey Andy, thanks for coming over. I just wanted to show you another feature of the Favorites Finder that you might find interesting."

We walk over to the Favorites Finder and Chris pulls up the screen that says 'Where Do You Want To Go?'

" I know how much you enjoy the Resource Center and have used it a lot. I wanted to show you a feature you may not be familiar with yet."

"You mean you realized you forgot to show me something important, right?"

Chris laughs, " Oh Andy, your confidence in me is so comforting. Now see this little square in the corner of the screen?"

I nod "Okay"

"If you pull this up, you have your family calendar. Now you already know that time has no meaning on this side, so there is no need for calendars on this side, right?"

"Right" I say hesitantly

"Wrong", he says emphatically. "This calendar is designed to keep you informed of upcoming events on Earth – which is locked into a time schedule. Or upcoming fantasies that are being planned on this side that may be of interest to you."

I look once again at Chris in confusion, knowing from experience not to open my mouth but to stay with him so he can explain.

"I wanted to show this to you today because,

as you can see here, your granddaughter Brooklynn Rose is getting married today and I thought you might want to check it out."

He smiles as I explode

"WHAT?! SHE'S WAY TOO YOUNG TO GET MARRIED! I DON'T WANT TO SEE THAT. WHY, HER DAD PROBABLY HAS A SHOT GUN OR SOMETHING! WHAT WAS KELLY THINKING RAISING HER KIDS LIKE THAT? THIS IS WAY TOO MUCH DRAMA FOR ME TO HAVE ANYTHING TO DO WITH, JOLY COW!!"

I pause as I notice Christopher is laughing to the point of nearly being in tears. I immediately have this sinking feeling that I have once again exploded into an emotional volcano prematurely.

"Andy, Andy, Andy. You seem to forget that time has no value on this side. A fantasy day for you on this side could use up ten years on the other side. Your granddaughter is a fine young lady who has found herself a fine young man. There is a lot of excitement in your family today and I thought you would like to see it."

I pause to catch my breath, and my sanity, I suppose.

"Oh. I can go to the wedding?"

Chris smiles patiently. "Yes. As an observer

only, of course. That's why I wanted to show you this feature. Many of your relatives come here to check the calendar out. Your dad likes to print it out as a newspaper and read up casually on what's happening. Why, it wouldn't surprise me if you saw your parents at the wedding today. And other relatives as well. Your family tree is full of romantics. Remember when Rosemary was having her tooth pulled and I told you how people often say they felt a closeness to their Dad at that moment. And how it's all because the hearts are connected?"

I shake my head as I'm beginning to see where this is going.

"That happens a LOT on big important days like a wedding and it's because so many family members on this side love to go to them. Their hearts are connected in love and it makes for a wonderful day for everyone. Again, you can only go as an observer, but what a great event. You can observe the whole thing and afterwards, if your parents or other relatives on this side are there, you can go to a bar like you did after your concert and celebrate the day!"

Wow! That sounds so very cool. I look at Chris and am almost certain that there are many questions I need to ask, but I certainly don't want to be late for my granddaughters wedding.

" Wow, I'm sure there's more to it, but I don't want to be late for the wedding. So I just go back to my room and fill out my sheet how?"

"Just put 'Today I'm Going To go to the other side and watch my granddaughter get married!' Then head out the door and enjoy!"

"Excellent! Thanks Chris." I pause and look at Chris, "So Brooklynn Rose is getting married today. Wow! My fantasies sure do use up a lot of time, don't they?"

Chris just smiles as I turn to head back to my room.

"And remember, they don't speak Latin down there."

I don't even respond except to throw up my arms in surrender. I have a wedding to get to.

I get inside and don't stop for anything. I don't want to miss one moment of this day on earth. I complete my paper, No names, 'Today I'm Going To go to the other side and watch my granddaughter get married!'

I head to the other door and open it with much anticipation. I see nothing but a brick wall in front of me.

"What the?!!!!" I scream in frustration! I

didn't check the messages. If it's Chris, I swear I'll kill him.

I bolt over to the blinking message box and push the button. This better be important!

"Hey Andy, your Mom and I and some other relatives are going to Brooklynn's wedding today. I'm sure you're probably already there, but if not why don't you join us!"

I take a deep breath of frustration as I turn to go back to the door. 'I am the grandfather of the bride and am the last one to know for crying out loud! I swear that Chris will be the death of me.'

I open the door to a beautiful setting. WOW. The decorations, the scenery, all the people dressed up so nicely.

Across the way I see my Dad waving his arm like a crazy man. Sure glad the 'earth people' can't see us that's for sure. I smile and head over where I find Mom, Dad and several others from my family tree. After a brief time of pleasantries, the music starts and we all give our full attention to the ceremony at hand.

My daughter, Kelly, the mother of the bride, is escorted in by her nephew Charlie, who appears to be one of the Groomsmen. How cool is that? They look so happy and eloquent.

As the Bridesmaids make their way down, I

notice Brooklynn's sister, Drew Isabella is the Maid of Honor! She looks so bright and beautiful!

I am so happy to see how my family has stayed together and seem so happy to be together. I notice one lady in the third row of seats keeps looking over my way. Hmmm. Me and the others from the 'other side' are pretty quiet, I think. I've only said 'wow' twenty times so far, but to my credit, I've been pretty quiet and actually humbled by all this. I'm wondering what 'wow' sounds like in Latin. ahhhh, I'm thinking too much. She's probably a psychic who talks to the dead or something. Maybe I should invite her out for a drink with the rest of us after the ceremony and really scare the hell out of her?

Then the music breaks and there at the back stands Ben and Brooklynn. My son-in-law looks so proud and strong. And I'm happy to see no shotgun! Brooklynn is just a beam of sunshine. As they walk down the aisle together I can hear that I am not the only 'other-sider' that is getting emotional, as sniffling seems to be the norm. Yes, there is crying in Heaven.

What a beautiful site. What a beautiful family. What a beautiful ceremony. I am so grateful to be able to be here for this and will make sure to check my calendar often from now on.

The ceremony was simply beautiful and as everyone heads for the reception, my Mom suggests we head back to our favorite watering hole on the other side and have a drink. Most of the other relatives decide to just go back to their rooms, but I'm happy to have Mom and Dad to myself in the bar after a special day like this.

"Sure glad you were able to join us Andy. You created quite a nice family down there."

"I know, really. It was good to see everyone together and happy. But my gosh, Brooklynn was so mature. Makes me wonder what all I've missed while I've been creating my fantasies." I say with a bit of annoyance at Chris not showing this feature to me before today.

"Ah, don't worry about that kid. It's all part of the deal up here. You'll get use to it. there's a button on the calendar that can show you past events that you can go to. Hell, your Mom and I spent a week in Paris. When we came back, the calendar tells me that Phillip's son's 5th birthday was today. We didn't even know he got married. I pushed the past events button and realized our week in Paris took up eight years on earth" He looks over and winks at Mom, "I could do another eight years like that though" Back to me, "We missed Phillips wedding, the birth of his two kids, Drew and Brooklynn's graduation from college, Charlie's draft into the big leagues and eventual call up to the Tigers. All in one week. That whole time thing can screw you up, but you eventually get use to it. You spend a day having a great week in Paris, then come back to the Fantasy Favorites and spend another day going to all the wonderful events you've missed over the past ten years on yesterday while you were in Paris for a week. If you think about it too much, it'll drive you nuts. The important thing to remember is that it all works in your favor. You don't miss out on anything because time means nothing on this side."

With that, I'm thinking it's time to turn in. But before I do, I ask my Dad, "Hey, did you notice that lady in the third row watching us? It was as if she could hear us or see us. Seemed kinda spooky to me?"

Dad and Mom both laugh before Dad replies, "Sure. You'll find that almost every time you go to an event down there, there is always one or two people who hear voices. Most of the 'earth people' think they are nuts, but they really aren't. We pretty much ignore them as they only hear Latin, so we really don't need to worry about it. But at a nice ceremony like a wedding, we really don't want to encourage it much either."

I am amused. "I guess next you'll be telling me that those Sci-Fi UFO shows are true."

"Well, Andy me boy, as you travel around the other worlds and see more through your fantasies, you'll learn that back on earth there is a very fine line between crazy and genius. There's a lot of stuff they think they have all figured out that are far off the mark. But there's a lot of things they are not far off with. It can be rather entertaining to watch some of those Sci-Fi shows once you know the truth on this side."

Wow. I've learned so much on this side, but mostly I've learned that with each day on this side, I have a lot more to learn.

I get back to my room and reflect on the wonderful day I've been given. I'm so glad that Kelly and Ben are having this great adventure in their life. I take comfort in knowing that Kelly was able to have that moment when she reflected with Ben that she felt a real closeness to her Dad today.

I know dear, I was with you. I was the one sniffling in Latin.

I lay my head down when suddenly, it hits me. I bolt up in my bed and scream, "CHARLIE PLAYS FOR THE DETROIT TIGERS?!?!?"?!?!"

I get up and bolt into the Resource Center only to find Chris in his usual boring posture at a table reading a book.

"WHY DIDN'T YOU TELL ME ABOUT CHARLIE PLAYING FOR THE TIGERS?!?! DID IT JUST SLIP YOUR MIND?!?! DID YOU NOT HAVE ENOUGH BRAINS TO THINK, 'GEE, CHARLIE'S GETTING CALLED UP TO THE DETROIT TIGERS TODAY. MIGHT BE SOMETHING ANDY- WHO BY THE WAY WANTED TO BE A BASEBALL PLAYER HIMSELF BUT HIS GIRLY CONSCIENCE, WHO KEPT CALLING ME AN IDIOT DIDN'T WANT HIM TO – MIGHT JUST WANT TO CHECK OUT!?!?

Chris looks up and smiles as if he were expecting me.

"Well if you recall, you were kind of in a hurry to get to Brooklynn's wedding. I pretty much figured when your parents were talking to you at the bar afterwards that you'd be back and I can show you some of the other features. Come on"

He stands up and heads for the Favorites

Finder. I just hate it when Chris is so emotionally lethargic when I explode like that.

"Now, remember this little box in the corner is where you can pull up your calendar, right?" He looks at me as I'm still glaring at him with less than heavenly eyes and knows he'll have to go on without me, knowing that I'll catch up eventually." Right. Well, you can set up your calendar any way you want. You can simply type in a name, let's say your daughter, Kelly." he types her name and the screen blinks. " The calendar will pull up all the info on Kelly that has occurred since the last time you checked. Since you are just learning this feature, of course, it will just generalize from the time you came to this side. You can pick any of the events listed and it will pull up a brief summary of the event. If the information is enough, you can move on to the next event. If you want to actually see how the event evolved, you can click on the play button and go into the Screening Room over there that I told you about and watch the whole story."

He looks at me and notices that I have regained my blood pressure and am now fully engaged with the conversation.

"Okay. Now here's a cool feature," he picks up

a thing that looks to me like a small microphone, " Follow me."

He goes over to the door and opens it. There are a couple of very nice comfortable seats in the room that also has a big screen like a movie theater, and I notice one of the seats has a very refreshing looking drink in the cup holder. I guess my guardian angel doesn't need a drink, I think with a tad measure of lingering contempt.

As Chris takes his seat, he continues, "This little gadget is called a MenuMic. It lets you bring the calendar in here so you can sit back and review all the events you want." he doesn't wait for a response from me, "Menu. Charlie. First day of Spring Training."

The screen lights up with a vision of Charlie getting out of his car.

"Nice car, Charlie boy."

As he gets his gear out of the trunk and heads into the clubhouse, Chris say "Stop"

"Hey, why did you stop it?" I ask Chris with disappointment as he ignores me and continues.

" I call this thing a MenuMic because you can use it to bounce around from event to event and see whatever parts you want. You don't really need this on this side, but I like to create things like this that will relate to your time frame on the other side so you can be more comfortable."

He looks at me with a smile, but again does not wait for a response.

"You have complete control over it. You can just see the highlights of a particular person – like Kelly- and stop at any time to review an event in her life with more detail.

Or say you want to check out Charlie's baseball career. You can start at his first Spring Training, then say 'STOP' and fast forward to his first at bat as a major leaguer, or go back to his college days and see what got him to that Spring Training camp. You're in control at all time. Like your Dad said, you can come back from a fantasy and spend a lot of time in here catching up with all the different events that have gone on while you were gone. The hardest part of this whole thing is getting to the point on this side where you can approach these fantasies without being controlled by the issue of time."

He hands me the MenuMic as he gets up and starts to the door as I consider what he has shown me.

As I get up to follow him out the door, I finally respond, "Man, by the time I get done reviewing all these events, half my family will be waiting at the Pearly Gates for me to come and greet them."

Chris stops. He doesn't look back at me, but instead bows his head and shakes it in bewilderment. "Let it go, Andy. Let ...... Time ...... Go......."

14

My Nineteenth Day

I get up fully rested after another great day of fulfilling fantasies. I seem to be getting into a rhythm with heaven. The biggest hurdle you have to get over is the issue of time – or on this side, the absence of time. Once you accept that time has no measurement here, you begin to relax more. I'm finding that I'm doing less 'planing' of fantasy days and instead just going with my heart each day I get up. It really does become a matter of simply taking each fantasy and embracing each moment of it without any concern for time. If you think too much, it will mess you up, and with each fantasy, I'm learning not to over think, but to simply trust, relax and make the most of every fantasy I take on.

As I'm sitting on my bed I notice my message light blinking. I check and it is Chris.

"Hey Andy, when you have a moment, come to the Resource Center. I have something you might be interested in."

I get up to go to the Resource Center smiling. I use to get so frazzled at the sound of Chris' voice when we both started this adventure, but now I appreciate that he really is looking out for my best interests. We've actually become good friends of sorts, yet I still love giving him attitude whenever I can, just for fun.

I go into the Resource Center and see Chris standing by the Favorites Finder.

"Thanks for coming, Andy."

"Well I didn't want to spend my day looking at a brick wall, ya know." I say with a tint of sarcasm.

Chris smiles and blows me off, " You could have gone ahead with a fantasy if you wanted. I would have left you that message every day until you responded. " He smiles at me, "I was completely confident you would get annoyed soon enough to come over and check this out."

He grabs the MenuMic and heads for the screening room as he continues.

" Remember when I told you about the Heart Program we have here?"

"Yea, the one where you can become someone's conscience to help them make better decisions or call them an idiot, right?"

"Right," as he opens the door, we both go into the screening room and take a seat.

"I have a situation here that might be a good opportunity for you to see how it works and the possibilities the program has."

"Okay." I don't challenge Chris as I use to. To be honest, I've been so busy doing my own fantasy thing that I haven't given the Heart Program much of a thought. It might be good to see what this is all about. If I've learned anything on this side, it's that everything is designed to have a positive outcome and increase the power of love, so I know that whatever it is Chris wants to show me is probably worth looking at.

We sit back as Chris speaks into the MenuMic, " Open Todd Flannery program."

The screen lights up with crashing music as we have clearly been transported into the middle of a pretty awesome music event. I'm not familiar with the band, but am not surprised. I don't even know what year it is down there. Regardless, I know good music when I hear it and this band has got it going tonight.

As the camera closes in on the lead singer, Chris says "Stop", and the action freezes.

"This is Todd Flannery. He's a very popular entertainer in the Country music world. Had a lot of hits, won some awards, made a ton of money. A really good guy."

" Well I hope you don't want me to give him voice lessons, because he sounds pretty good to me," I say with a smile.

"No, music is not an issue with Todd. On the outside, he appears to be in pretty good shape, but his heart gives us a critical reading that concerns us. We need someone special to become his conscience and hopefully help him choose the best path."

" What's the issue?" I ask, somewhat curious as to why Chris would think I might be that 'someone special' to handle this.

"You spent a lot of time in the music business and understand that being an entertainer isn't as glamorous and wonderful as people think."

I chuckle, "That's why I just wanted to be a writer. I wanted no part of being on stage and all the headaches that come with it."

"Exactly. You understand all the sacrifices Todd had to make to get to the level of entertainment that he's been able to obtain. Those sacrifices add up and can become a real source of frustration for an entertainer. A review of Todds heart shows us that his frustration level is getting to a critical level and we feel it is vital that we get a strong person who can relate to the critical choices that have to be made if love is going to win."

I raise my eyebrows in a mix of horror and humor, "Well you certainly have my attention now, Chris! I can't imagine why you would think of me over all the others on this side to be the perfect 'special someone' to be a conscience of a Country Music superstar in a critical time in his career!? Was Johnny Cash not available?"

Chris smiles and delights in my contributions to the conversation.

" You would be perfect because you have a passion for the three critical elements in this situation. You love the music business and already understand why Todds heart would be so frustrated. You loved baseball and always wanted to be a baseball player."

"Excuse me?" I'm taken back as Chris has said

nothing about baseball before this. Chris just smiles as he continues.

"And you were exceptional in this area." he turns back to the screen and says, "Corey Flannery"

The screen flashes to a baseball field where I see a young ballplayer diving for a ground ball and making one of the best plays I've ever seen.

"WOW! Who's that kid?"

"That's Todd's son. Plays for Vandy and is projected to be one of the first players picked in the major league draft. He's got it all. Kind of reminds me of Derek Jeter. And a really good kid. He'd be a great pick up for any major league team. Can't miss with this kid."

"Okay. So what's the story?" I ask, starting to get the impression that Chris – again – knows what he is doing.

"Well, the story is Todd's heart. Todd loves his life as an entertainer. Loves his music. Loves the people he works with. The whole thing. But he's getting to that age where he's starting to realize the price he paid in his private life in order to have his music. He's been around the entertainment business long enough to see many of his friends in the business struggle with broken relationships in their family. He can see it in his wife's eyes and in her voice when he is home. He can see it in his son on those rare times when he is able to make a game or important event. He wrestles with the thought of having to choose between his music and those people he loves the most and is frustrated at knowing that in his business, there really aren't too many options."

"I've heard that story many times before, Chris, and it always makes me thankful that God only gave me the talent to write." I say with a smile of gratitude.

"Yes, but what made you so special was your ability to walk away from your keyboard to go see your daughters track meet, or cheerleading, or soccer games. Your passion for writing was strong, but you sacrificed many opportunities to take steps in turning that passion into a wonderful career because your passion for family was even greater. Everybody has to make sacrifices. Everybody has to make choices, Andy. I chose you for this job because you were one of those rare people that had the ability to make the choice of your heart. I chose you because the sacrifices you made were with your writing so you could be a good Dad and not the other way around. And that's one of the main reasons you got through the wash as easily as you did. I chose you because you would be perfect."

I sit back and think about it. It does sound intriguing to be sure. I look at Chris who has that smile that tells me there's more.

"And Andy, I saved the best for last."

Oh brother. Again my eyebrows elevate in a painfully questioned posture.

"O....kay"

" You might be interested to know who Corey's great-grandfather was."

I lean towards Chris in reluctant anticipation. "Gooooooo.....On..."

" You may know him. Corey's great-grandfather was a guy named Tim Flannery."

I slump back in my chair in disbelief. "NO WAY!!! The San Diego Padres Tim Flannery?!?"

Chris smiles, "The very same one. The Tim Flannery you wrote a column for in the San Diego Tribune calling on the Padres to retire his number because he was a true Padres who represented the city so well. The same Tim Flannery who told Trader Jack that if he traded him, he would retire because he only played baseball so he could surf during the day, The same Tim Flannery that you helped out when you worked in the music business to make sure he was getting his royalties for his CD. Todd's father was Tim's son."

"WOW" is the only response I can muster.

"When the Angels had our meeting to go over the Heart Program and discuss the needs for those on Earth who are in a critical situation, I heard this story about Todd and knew I just had to get you involved. There is no question that if you're working as Todds conscience, I'd be going to the next meeting with everyone showering me with accolades for my choice to have you be Todds conscience." he pauses and smiles at me, "You owe me at least that for all the grief you gave me when you first came through the wash, ya know."

I bolt up, "NOT FAIR! You earned most of that, pal!" I say with a smile as he laughs. I pause and sit back to consider his proposal. "What would I do?"

"The key to being a good conscience is learning to separate your 'thinking' and your 'speaking' When you 'speak', you literally become that voice in their head. But whatever you 'think' stays as your own thoughts. Remember that conscience you complained about because she was a female and kept calling you an idiot? "

I look at Chris with a bracing hesitance.

"We had to remind her many times that it's OKAY to 'think' that but don't say it all the time because you were getting pretty frustrated at constantly hearing 'You're an idiot'."

"Well, ya gotta admit she wasn't a very good conscience." I say with a sense of smugness as Chris jumps in to break up the smug.

"Oh contraire my good man. She is still one of our best conscience workers we call on. When she lived on the other side, she was very outspoken and not afraid to speak her mind to anyone . We find those people make the best conscience workers on this side. Once she learned to separate her 'thinking' from her 'speaking', she was able to create her 'voice' within her clients in a strategically critical time to get the best results." He pauses, but jumps in again before I can say anything. "And don't think for a moment she didn't do a good job with you. She gets a lot of the credit for you being able to turn away from your writing and go watch your girls perform. She is an excellent conscience worker."

I snicker as I lean back in my chair, "Well when you are called an idiot that many times, you're bound to figure things out, I guess."

I look over to Chris who is just smiling and gives a nod that suggests he wouldn't be challenging that comment any time soon.

"So if I do this, what is the event coming up that I need to be aware of?"

Chris smiles, "Oh there are no events we are looking at. We don't look down the road to the future events on the horizon. We look at the heart, and Todd's heart tells us that he is in a critical moment in his journey that requires someone like you to work with him. Remember, people down there have free will and so it's not important to us what events are coming up with them, it's only important that we have the right conscience in place who can handle whatever situation comes up in the best interest of love. It's important that we have the right worker to turn whatever situation comes into a positive victory for love. I will say that most workers who come back after a successful assignment in the Heart Program are always blown away at the experience. I think this would be an excellent opportunity for you to get a feel for the program. And remember, you can at any time abort the assignment if it's not working out for you. This is your heaven to create as you will. I think it's a perfect match for you, but if you don't, then don't take it."

Chris has got me thinking now. It does sound like a great opportunity and he is right that all the elements are areas I was so passionate about. It would be nice to take a break from all my selfish fantasy filling and give this a try. Who knows, maybe this would open up a lot more opportunities for me to create my fantasies.

"Well Chris, I have to admit that it sounds interesting and although I'm 100% hesitant, I'm really leaning towards giving it a shot. If it doesn't work out for me with all these elements I'm so passionate about, at least I'll know that the Heart Program isn't for me, right?"

"Exactly! But I'm thinking you're going to be so good at this that you're going to come back and ask me if there's any Opera singers needing help." He smiles as I slump.

" Ha....Ha... Ha .... Well, listen pal, if this kid gets drafted by the Dodgers, I am going to abort immediately. And you better not let Timmy know where to find me, that's for sure."

Chris breaks into laughter. I do as well.

"So what do I need to do?" I ask.

"Are you sure you want to try this?"

"I'm not going to face any brick walls, am I?"

Chris laughs, "No, there are no brick walls in this assignment. You just have to remember that you can think whatever you want, but if you speak, Todd will hear that as his' voice'. I'll be able to speak to you just as you are able to speak to Todd, so if you don't want to hear from me, you better keep it clean" He says with a smile.

I hesitate in thought for a brief moment, then boldly announce, "Let's do this!"

Suddenly I am looking out of a car going up a driveway to what is one niiiiiice house. I look over and have no idea who the driver is, but I do notice that I am looking out Todds eyes. I feel like I am connected to his heart as I feel a sense of nervousness in his spirit. I can 'hear' everything he is thinking. In an instant, I feel as if I've been with Todd forever and am amazed at how quickly I feel up to speed with him and fully aware of what is going on with him.

The driver speaks, "You know Todd, I didn't want to tell you around all the others but I found out this morning that when they announce the CMA nominations tomorrow, You are going to be nominated for Entertainer of the Year award." He looks over at Todd with a big smile.

"Really? Wow! That's one award I've never

been nominated for. Wow! Guess it has been a pretty good year for us."

"You can tell Donna and Corey, but don't call anyone else. CMA gets a little frisky when everyone knows before they announce. They just let me know so they can line up any interviews for the media tomorrow. You'll be here, right?"

Todd looks at his home, "You bet I will. Just make sure we only have a short time set aside in the afternoon for the media. I've been on the road for a bit and want to be alone with Donna."

"No problem, bud. Go have a nice evening with your wife. Give her my best. I'll give you a shout around noon to set everything up."

Todd gets out of the car and is greeted by Donna at the front door, as the car makes it's way out of the driveway. They embrace in a very warm hug accompanied by a rather passionate kiss. Man, I know I'm just his conscience, but boy am I burning up from the heat coming out of his heart!

Todd and Donna have a very warm night of catching up and drinking wine in front of the fireplace. I'm beginning to wonder just how much this guy needs me as his conscience. I haven't seen or heard anything that would indicate that this guy has a heart in a critical level of frustration, that's for sure.

Todd brings back another glass of wine, hands one to Donna and sits close by her.

"Larry told me as I was getting out of the car that the CMA people called him to see if I'd be available tomorrow." he says smiling.

"Oh..... Realllly?" says Donna, liking the sound of this conversation.

Todd tips his glass with hers as he continues, "How does Entertainer of the Year sound to you?"

Donna screams out loud and nearly spills her wine all over the both of them.

"Get out of here. Oh honey, that's so great!" as she clumsily sets her wine on the table and wraps her arms around Todd, "You've worked so hard for so long. It's about time they recognize what you do for your fans. I'm so proud of you!"

Another long embrace with a passionate kiss ensues.

The next couple of days are pretty routine for me. I'm starting to think maybe Chris doesn't have a great handle on the human race, as I've been the conscience of this guy for almost a week now and not once have I had to say anything as 'the voice' of his conscience –

though I admit I almost blew it the other night when Donna was getting a little 'frisky' again and I almost blurted out, "Hey Pal, give it a rest, already" But to my credit, I caught myself before speaking as I understood that the voice of his conscience should never come from MY voice of jealousy.

Point is, I'm not feeling such a critical time for this guy. He really does seem like a really good guy who loves his music and his wife. From what I can see and hear, Todd seems to be a lock for the Entertainer of the Year award, and call me crazy, but I'm just not feeling a lot of critical frustration for this guy. I feel like I'm just a quiet voice along for the ride of this wonderful story of life.

After a day of golf – clearly, this guy doesn't need a conscience for his golf game, I had to cover my mouth after almost every shot! This guy is great and I have made a mental note to talk to Chris about the unfairness of God giving so much talent in so many areas to some people, yet only gives me talent to be a 'nice' writer of little noteworthiness! A few interviews and stopping by one of his favorite charities he likes to partner with, Todd comes home to find Donna putting together what appears to be a rare, quiet dinner for just the two of them.

After a warm hug and kiss and review of his day, Todd goes to pour himself a glass of wine.

"I was thinking that we should go out to a nice place for lunch on the day of the CMA awards. That night's going to be pretty crazy and we probably won't have a chance to eat much before or after the ceremony." He looks at her as she smiles and winks at him.

"That sounds good. What day is that? I haven't put it on the calendar yet."

She dries her hands with a towel as she heads over to the desk with a calendar on it.

"June 8th. I think it's a Sunday night?"

She looks at her calendar and you can almost sense the life in her heart being sucked out of her and being replaced by a numbness as she just glares down at the calendar.

"Is there a problem?" Todd says, sensing the mood has quickly gone south.

Donna goes back to her cooking, desperately trying to calm the emotional screaming of silence, "No. It's fine. Wherever you want to go would be great. It's going to be a big night for you."

Todd has been married to this woman long

enough to see through that statement as he heads over to the calendar to see for himself. He looks down at June 8th and his heart sinks. It is circled with an arrow pointing to the side where a note reads: MLB DRAFT.... PARTY HERE ..... TELL DAD.... at that moment, Todd's heart is exploding with alarms that has quickly thrown me out of my casual posture and into a frantic state of panic.

Todd turns to his wife, "The baseball draft is the same night?"

Her hesitance to say anything says enough as Todd desperately looks for words to break the silence. I am in absolute panic mode now, not knowing if I should abort. Say something to Todd. Or if so, WHAT?!?!"

"THAT SUCKS!!!" I say out loud before I cover my mouth desperate not to say anything further.

"That Sucks" says Todd

I gasp. I guess he heard me. Oh my God. Am I responsible for how he handles this? Is it up to me to solve this dilemma for Todd and Donna? I start scrambling for an answer, fully aware that I have NO CLUE what to tell this guy as my confidence level gets dangerously close to just aborting and forgetting this whole Heart Program stuff.

Donna slaps me back to the moment.

"It's okay, Todd. Corey knows how much your music means to you and of course, he'll understand what a big night this is for you too. He wanted to have the party here instead of the dorm at school because we are nearby and he thought it'd be cool. It's no big deal. You both will have a great night for sure, and that's what counts."

"BAD ANSWER!!!!" I say as I jump up furious and immediately slap my hands over my mouth. Oops. But almost as quickly remove my hands to continue. "No! No! It's NOT okay! You had a choice between music and baseball, and you chose music. Corey only wanted baseball, pal, and this is a big moment for him!!!" I take a deep breath and gather myself a bit. Then, in a more gentle tone continue, "Listen, I know you may have to miss this event too. But don't think for a minute that IT'S OKAY . It's not okay. No matter how you look at it, it's NOT OKAY! He's your SON!"

Todd goes over to Donna and wraps his arms around her. He's finding it difficult to find the words to satisfy his troubled heart.

"You know it gets harder and harder to say no

to you and Corey. As I get older, I'm finding it hard to accept that it's all worth it."

Donna turns and puts her arms around his neck. The look in her eyes absolutely melts my heart. I can see that love is certainly not an issue for these two. Donna is clearly the rock of this family and there is no doubt that in my role here, I am fighting as much for this great lady as I am for Todd.

" Honey, we've raised Corey well. He understands the importance of following your passions and I have reminded him many times that whatever your passion is, there will always be a price to pay in order to achieve the most from your passions. Everybody has a passion, but so few actually end up living their passions." she pauses to give Todd a kiss before continuing, " I have two men in my life who have lived, and will continue to live the best of what their passionate hearts have created. Don't think for a moment that I don't go to bed every night thinking that I am the luckiest woman alive."

Another kiss.

I am dumbfounded. WOW! What a great woman. I could not have said it any better. But I am still compelled to get in the last word. "She's right of course. But don't think for a minute that it's okay. I don't know what the answer is, but make no mistake about it. Missing your sons draft party will... NEVER ..... BE ..... OKAY!'

Todd takes a sip of his wine as Donna turns to attend to the dinner again. He turns away to go get ready for dinner when he turns once again towards Donna.

"You're a good woman, Donna. I suppose there is no easy answer for June 8th for sure. But I could never live with myself if I didn't trust that you understand that in my heart, it will NEVER be okay when it comes to saying no to my family. It will NEVER be okay."

Donna looks out the window, unable to look at Todd, "I know Todd" she says with a loyal smile and watering eyes.

For the next several days there is not much for me to say. Todd is doing a lot of thinking and soul searching and I can tell that he is really troubled by this whole June 8th issue. I feel for him, but I am also quick to speak up whenever his thinking starts going down the path of justifying the situation as no big thing. It is what it is. They know how the music business is and it's just an unfortunate scheduling problem that we'll all have to live with. We all need to just get over it.

For the first time, I have a much deeper appreciation for the female conscience I had that got in trouble so much for calling me an idiot. Not only am I feeling a sense of payback time in the use of my commentaries with Todd, but I'm actually having fun with it. Sometimes he gets a little smug in his thinking that it's all okay and I'll just shout out, "BULLSHIT!" without any apologies

["ANDY, THIS IS CHRIS: PLEASE REMEMBER YOU REPRESENT LOVE AND I"D REALLY LIKE YOU TO STOP SAYING THAT PLEASE!!"]

Sometimes, I'll gently whisper in his ear, "You're an idiot" when I feel his confidence isn't that strong in justifying his acceptance – just like MY conscience use to do to me

And sometimes I just love to sit back and blurt out "WRONG!" every time Todd goes over his lists of justifications until he gets annoyed enough to shake his head and tells himself he's over thinking this and he needs to concentrate on the here and now.

In fact the only troubling thing I face is Chris yelling in my ear every time my phraseology get's a little too colorful for him. This is emotional stuff. He can't expect me to be Mr.

Clean every time I open my mouth for crying out loud.

We get to a few days before the CMAs and I find Todd in Larry's office going over all the protocol for the big night. So many things to go over to make sure there are no mishaps. Todd is a little annoyed. He loves being on the road playing his music, but a lot of the reason is that he's in charge. It's his show and he controls everything that goes on. With an awards show, he seems to be told by too many others what he has to do. Where he has to sit, what time he has to go to the bathroom, everything choreographed without ever asking him what HE wants to do. He's never been a big fan of these award shows, but understands in the entertainment business the last thing you want to do is create too many enemies. There are people who don't even know you that can make your ability to make music a living hell, and as a good entertainer does, you simply learn to smile and play along at these things.

Larry pauses in the discussion and confronts Todd.

"You okay, buddy? You seem a bit distracted " he says.

Of course I laugh to myself – careful not to

blurt out anything at this point- Distracted? My God, Todd's an entertainer and Larry's a businessman .... of course he's distracted, you idiot.... I'm so bored listening to your mechanical sermon of worthless award show protocol that it's all I can do to keep myself from aborting this assignment due to sheer boredom.

"It's all good. It's just an award show."

"Just an award show? Why you have a chance to become the Entertainer of the Year ! That's a huge honor that many don't have in this business. I would think you'd be a little more excited."

"Yea, well you know I'm not that big on award shows. It's an honor for sure and I know I have to play along and all. But my career choice was to play my music for people, which I love to do. Going to these fancy award shows where everyone dresses up and pats each other the back has never been my thing." he pauses, then continues, "You know the major league draft is Sunday night too, right?"

Larry sits back as now he gets it. "Oh, so that's what's eat'n you? Hey don't worry about that. I'm sure Corey will do very well. You'll both be big winners on Sunday and that's the main thing. That's what you should be excited about.

Hell, I'll make sure we have someone plugged into the draft to let you know what team he's going to before you accept your award. How cool would that be to dedicate your award to your son who just got drafted by the Dodgers?"

I get a little emotional when I hear the word Dodgers and this guy has just crossed the line with me. I'm not sitting quiet any more!

"NO WAY, PAL!!!!!!! Don't listen to this guy. How many kids does he have playing in the major leagues, huh? He's just a yes boy who knows if you play the game right, he'll be making even more money down the road. He doesn't care about family! Do what you gotta do, but don't do it for THIS guy. He's an idiot!"

"Well he's looking to go first or second and he's having a big get-together at our house to watch it. I'd rather be there than at some fancy awards show."

"Oh he'll understand, Todd. Heck, how many guys get drafted into the big leagues and never even make it to the Majors? He'll understand. And when you show up for his first major league at bat, nobody will remember his draft party."

"I CALL BULLSHIT!!!! Who does this guy think he is? Is he going to guarantee that you'll be at Corey's first major league at bat? Listen pal, you're going to be sitting in a rocking chair someday looking back at all the missed opportunities to be a Dad because that's ALL you'll have to look back on. MISSED OPPORTUNITIES! And where will this blowhard be? Probably kissing up to some new talent that he can make a bunch of money off without ONE SINGLE THOUGHT ABOUT YOU OR COREY!!!"

[Andy, this is Chris: Again....PLEASE be careful with your words]

"Well I'm just saying it's an awards show. I get excited about my fans and my music. Award shows are just a side bar that has to be done, but for the most part it's more important to people like you. I already get my award every night I perform and can look down at the people in the front row and see that the $200 bucks they spent was the best $200 bucks they spent all year. And I don't have to wear a tux for that."

I like it. Todd made a good argument and I can't help but think my ranting in his ear helped to push him a little.

"Ahhh, don't worry about it Todd. We'll have a great night Sunday night. You can go home and help your son celebrate his future and it will all be worth it on Monday morning, you'll see. We can go over this again tomorrow. Go home and be with your family."

Todd gets up to leave, "Well, you know if I had a choice, there is no way I'd pass up the draft for an awards show."

"If there was a choice, I'd give it to you, Todd. It's the music business. Ya gotta be there when they're passing out the love. It's not a choice."

With that, the frustrated Todd leaves. I sit back emotionally drained. I really feel for the guy. I know his heart and also know that what Larry says is pretty much the way the music business world works. You don't snub the academy when they nominate you for Entertainer of the Year, that's for sure.

As we are heading home, Todds mind is going way faster than his car. He's really wrestling with it and I feel an energy in his heart that makes me pause. It's almost as if he's left a small window of hope open. Should I say something? What can I say?

As he pulls into his garage he finally concludes that Larry is right. There simply is no other way.

But I decide to have the last word, " Listen, you know that Corey's name is going to be called out Sunday night. You could sit in the arena all night in your fancy tux and never hear your name called out. Will it be worth it then?”

We are at a very nice restaurant where Todd and Donna are enjoying a late afternoon lunch. Todd seems a little more upbeat than he has the past few weeks.

Donna notices.

“You seem relaxed today. It’s good to see.”

Todd looks lovingly into her eyes, “It’s going to be a great night tonight.”

“I know it’s been rough on you with the Draft and the CMAs on the same night. I’m glad you’re at a point of accepting it as just another part of the deal. Corey has also come to accept it as well.” she pauses and then lightens up, “Hell, I’m the one who should be pouting! I want to be at both events and SHOULD be there for the men in my life!”

As they are getting into their car to leave, Todd’s phone rings.

“ Hey, Joe. Were you able to work things out?”

He listens with a growing smile.

“Excellent. I appreciate you pulling the strings for me pal. I owe you one.”

With that, he puts the phone up and heads down the road as Donna inquires about the call.

“Who’s Joe?’

"An old friend who works at the studio. He helped me put together a little something for the show tonight."

Donna looks at him with a warm smile, "This is going to be such a special night."

Todd looks over at her smiling, "It sure is, honey. It sure is."

They leave the restaurant and after a few turns, Donna becomes a little concerned, "Did you forget something at home?"

Todd smiles broadly, "Yes. Yes, I did."

"Will we have enough time?"

"Donna, my beautiful wife, we are parents. We never have enough time."

Donna smiles unaware of the meaning of his comment.

As he pulls into the drive, Donna says, "Oh good, Corey's already here with some of his friends."

As the garage door opens, Todd drives in as Donna speaks up, "Why are you pulling into the garage. We don't have much time before the show?"

"I know. We better get in there." he looks to Donna with a big, loving smile.

Donna sits bewildered as it's becoming clear what is going on.

Todd walks into the house from the garage to find Corey and many of his friends hovered around the TV. Corey sees his Dad.

"Dad! What are you doing here? Why aren't you at the CMAs?"

Todd is loosening his tie, "Well, ya know Corey, there's no guarantee that they're going to call my name tonight, but you and I know your name will be called. Why would I sit in an arena in this stuffy tuxedo listening to a bunch of other people's name being called out when I could be here knowing that my sons name is going to be called and the party will begin!?"

Corey and Todd embrace as Donna stands behind with tears rolling down her face.

Behind them, the TV announces, "The first choice in the 2051 major league draft for the Seattle Mariners is Vanderbilt shortstop Corey Flannery"

The house explodes with screams and high-fives as Todd holds Corey with no signs of letting go. Finally he steps back with tears rolling down his eyes, "Well, son, looks like I'll have to be booking a lot more tours in the northwest in the coming years."

He high-fives his son and starts towards the gathering, "Okay why do I see people without a drink, here? Com'on, let's get this party going! We've all just become Seattle Mariners fans!!"

Everyone screams!!

Meanwhile, at the arena where the CMA award show is going on, we hear the announcement, "And the Entertainer of the Year award goes to .... Todd Flannery"

The crowd breaks into a guarded applause as the buzz all night was that Todd was a no-show. Some even booed his absence.

"Ladies and Gentlemen, Todd Flannery is unable to be with us tonight but made the following video."

The lights go down and the screen lights up with Todd sitting in a recording studio behind a microphone with his guitar hanging behind him. He is holding a picture – facing in- on his lap.

"I'd like to thank the Academy for this tremendous honor you have given me tonight. Please know that my absence there in no way reflects the feeling I have of being called the Entertainer of the Year when the Academy has so many great entertainers to choose from.

"But I'm not with you tonight because there is – if I may be honest with you – a greater award for me right here." he turns the picture around and it is Corey in his Vandy uniform.

"This is my son Corey who has worked so hard to become one of the most sought after college baseball players in the country. Tonight was the major league draft and my son was the first pick, going to the Seattle Mariners. I would never want to miss this moment in my sons life and I hope you understand. It is a huge honor, of course, to be called the Entertainer of the Year. But it is even a greater honor to be called the Dad of number 7 for the Seattle Mariner's."

"Thanks again."

The arena starts a polite applaud that builds with the crowd standing in respect, some wiping tears from their eyes.

Meanwhile, back at the homestead, the crowd explodes into another celebration as they have moved over to the CMA awards after Corey went so early.

Corey hugs his Dad. "How did you know I was going to Seattle?"

Todd looks a bit disappointed at the question, "Hey, I'm the Entertainer of the Year, ya know. I've got some connections."

"You got someone from Seattle to tell you before the draft?" Corey asks

Todd laughs out loud, "NO! Joe and I did it the other day in his studio. We did a video for any team with a marginal interest in drafting you. He was at the awards show tonight to make sure they played the right one. The only concern I had was if the Padres traded up to snag you… they were one of the few teams we felt had no chance."

Corey laughs, "That's so cool!" He pauses and looks at his Dad. "Thanks Dad. For everything. I Love you."

They embrace in another warm hug when suddenly I am transported into the Resource Center where I find Chris holding a hanky with tears running down his face. He doesn't hesitate to leap into my arms.

"I knew you could do it! That was AWESOME!! I knew you were the right guy for the job! I KNEW you'd get them straightened out! That was a GREAT victory for love you just pulled off, pal!   That   was AWWWWWWSOMMMMMMMME!!!"

Why, my guardian angel has gone bazurk! He's running around giving high-fives to bookshelves for crying out loud! I've never seen Chris exhibit any emotions since I've been here, but he's absolutely gone mad tonight!

I sit down at a table that has a drink already set up for me. I take a sip as I marvel at Chris running around like a lunatic, waiting to see what I should do now.

Finally Chris is ready to take a break and comes to sit at the table.

"Man, we could not have asked for a better result than that, Andy! Thank you so much. The light of love is shining ten times brighter tonight because of you! Thank you, thank you, thank you." He takes a deep breath and gathers some of his composure. "So, what do you think of the Heart Program?"

I laugh openly, " Well it certainly showed me a side of my Guardian Angel that I haven't seen before, that's for sure."

"Oh Andy, trust me. All the guardian angels will go crazy when we get together again and review this case. You really did do a great job, Andy. I really do appreciate your help in this situation."

"Well it was good for me too, Chris. It really was a great feeling when Todd called to set up the recording session and I knew he was going to make the right choice. I could see myself taking another assignment from time to time."

We get up to conclude this 'day', absolutely spent by the emotional energy consumed in getting this victory for Love.

"Just let me know how Corey turns out, okay?"

"You can check it yourself on the calendar. There's a conscience worker file where you can look up anyone you worked with to see how they're doing. Be sure to schedule Corey's first major league game."

"Will do. And you let me know if you need anything else, alright."

"I do have an Opera singer and a Dodger that needs some Love." He bursts into laughter as I head through the door for a good nights rest.

I sit on my bed and reflect about what an experience I had with this Heart Program. I'm really glad I did this and can really see the possibilities it has. I'm certain that I will participate in this program again, but for now, I think I'll take a break. It's a nice program, but it's also a very emotional program. I'm thinking it would be really good on a now and then bases as a break from my fantasy creating. Chris says there are some who do nothing but the Heart Program. I couldn't do that. But it is a great feeling when it turns out as well as this one did.

It's then I notice my message light is blinking. I turn it on.

"Andy, Tim Flannery here. I just really wanted to thank you for what you've done for my family.

Todd's a good boy and I was so happy to see how you were able to steer him to the right choices. I owe you a one, mu friend. I'll make sure to let you know when Corey's first big league game is. We can go together and have a great time! Until then, Thanks again. I really do appreciate what you did."

Wow! My baseball hero from my youth on the other side just invited me to hang with him at a baseball game and watch his great-grandson play for the Seattle Mariners. As I lay down, I'm thinking this Heart Program has a lot of potential.

As I start to fade, my heart is smiling. What a day

The End - Really

no... really, I'm done ....

No wait ..... what if.....

NO!!!.....

Step away from the keyboard....

But...

Stop hanging around MY Heaven and go create your own days in Heaven!

And let me know what YOUR best day in Heaven would be!

Go to my website, www.TKRwriteNOW.com and 'contact me'

Give me 'Your Best Day in Heaven' .... who knows, if I get enough, maybe I'll create another book,

"Your First 7Days in Heaven"